KING OF WRATH

LORDS OF LAS VEGAS

TAMMY ANDRESEN

❀ Created with Vellum

STALK ME LIKE AN ALPHA!

Join my newsletter to get all the latest updates!

Tammy's Newsletter

And follow me everywhere else for teasers, giveaway, book news and fun!

www.authortammyandresen.com
www.facebook.com/authortammyandresen
www.instagram.com/tammyandresen
https://www.tiktok.com/@lordsoflasvegas
www://amazon.com/authortammyandresen

KING OF WRATH

A young woman with a dark secret.
A calculating billionaire, the enemy of her father.

JAKE

Cruel.
    Cunning.
    Ruthless.
    A beast in disguise.

My family rules Vegas with an iron fist and when another family crosses us… As the patriarch of my family, I have been chosen as the instrument of revenge. It's a job I relish.

The prize I'm after… the mob boss's youngest daughter, Nia.

As beautiful as she is sought after, I'm certain she knows her father's darkest secrets and she's the key to his undoing.

The only question is how to get my little songbird to sing?

As sweet as she is innocent, she wants to be good.

But I'm older, wiser, hard as they come. She's no match for me...

I see the way her pupils dilate, and her breath hitches every time I'm near. I know the truth. She wants me.

So how am I going to convince Nia to betray her family, her father?

There is only one weapon for this salacious battle.

Seduction.

NIA

My family could only dream of having the power and success of the Kincaids. Why my father tried to challenge them, I don't know, and I don't want to.

The only thing I want from this life is to get out.

But my plans are ruined when my father can't make good on his debts and the Kincaids send their most devilish weapon: Jake Kincaid.

Instead of leaving, I find myself smack in the middle of their war. Two men hardened by years of fighting.

On one side, my cruel, manipulative father. The other... Jake Kincaid, a lion on the prowl. I shouldn't want him, but the attraction that pulls at me is electric.

I won't be my father's pawn and I won't give in to this crazy desire for Jake.

So, I run.

But Jake Kincaid is a beast of a man. A predator. And what do predators do?

They chase their prey...

CHAPTER ONE

Nia

Deep inside I keep a dark secret. It's so ugly and awful, it has colored my entire life.

I stare out at the perfectly manicured lawn of my gated home, the lush, green grass and sunshine mocking my mood.

I pull my long blonde hair back into a high ponytail, feeling a bit of air on my neck as I hum a bluesy song meant to remind me of why sunshine isn't always happy. If it was, Las Vegas would never be sad, but I swear, it's one of the most morally bankrupt places on Earth.

I have proof. Everyone thinks my mother's death was an accident. A drunken drowning in her own tub. As if that isn't dark enough.

But the truth is, the man who is publicly acknowledged as my father killed her. And he did it because he learned the truth about me.

I'm not his daughter.

I used to be his favorite. His namesake. Now, it's all just a careful façade. He pretends to love me, and I pretend that the very sight of him doesn't make me recoil in revulsion.

If I don't...I'm sure I'll be the next accidental death.

But privately, I'm making plans. I'm going to leave Vegas, disappear.

I've got it all mapped out.

I just need the right moment, the right person, and then I'll be gone. What comes after I leave, I couldn't say. That's the next problem.

"Nia," my sister Jess calls. "Are you ready yet? We're leaving in like fifteen minutes."

I push up from my chair on the covered patio, stepping into the much-cooler house. "I'll be ready. Just give me five."

She snorts. "No shower?"

I roll my eyes. Jess is a girly girl. It's hair and makeup for hours. I only wear the barest bit of mascara and gloss, my hair usually pulled into a ponytail like it is now or down in my loose, natural waves. "Of course I'm going to shower."

Not that I care about how I look or smell for this particular outing. We have a weekly date with a few girlfriends at our father's casino, the Diamond.

They all like it because we drink for free. My father likes it because he can keep an eye on us. I don't give a crap about socializing, but it's all part of the charade. I pretend to be the frivolous daughter of the successful Vegas casino owner. He pretends to care. Neither are true.

I don't care about the money or the big house. I'd happily live in a tiny apartment if it meant I was free.

And Toni Carcetti isn't a success. I know how to discreetly listen, and Toni is about to lose several properties. He's distracted. It's the chance I've been waiting for.

But if I'm going to successfully escape, I'm going to need some cover. The only person who might be able to help me is Jess.

Not that she wants to escape. She loves Vegas and this life. Granted, she doesn't know the truth, but I'm not sure she'd believe me even if I presented her with a mountain of evidence.

She's happy being a mafia princess.

Or maybe I stopped being able to trust anyone a long time ago.

Either way, if she's going to help me, she'll have to do it unknowingly. Shouldn't be a problem.

I run up to my room and take a two-minute shower, changing into a strappy sundress that hugs my curves.

My mom was a beauty. We look a lot alike, except for my blonde hair. I'm surprised Toni didn't question my paternity sooner. I'm the only blonde in the entire Carcetti family. Today, I let my hair fall around my shoulders in loose waves, putting on the mascara and lip gloss that are my regulars.

Then I'm back downstairs.

Jess shakes her head when she sees me, her lip curling.

She's had a bunch of work done and she hates that I don't put more effort into my appearance. "It's not fair," she snorts now. "You shouldn't look that good when you don't try at all."

I shrug as I walk past her heading for the car. "Who are we meeting tonight?"

"Renee and Justine," she answers, falling in step next to me. "Casandra isn't coming."

"How come?"

Jess rolls her eyes. "Didn't you hear? Mason Kincaid got married."

I'm trying to keep up. "Okay?"

"Casandra was holding a torch for the King of Vegas," Jess whispers. "She's too depressed to go out."

I shake my head. Casandra didn't really know Mason Kincaid, she'd only seen him from afar, met him at a few charity events that are a part of the façade we all wear. But her lack of a real relationship didn't stop her from talking about him constantly. "Really? Married?"

"That's right. Daddy says that's why the Kincaids are calling in so many debts. They want to protect Mason's new bride. Isn't it romantic?"

I barely keep from rolling my eyes. "Did you mean psychotic?"

"What's wrong with a man protecting the woman he loves?"

"Potato, potahto," I mutter, sure Jess won't understand. To protect her, the new Queen of Vegas, they are going to hurt a whole bunch of people. Jess is seeing herself as the protected woman but we're about to be the bugs the Kincaids squash. I'm sure of it.

"You know the Kincaid who is really hot," she sighs, as the car pulls up, ignoring the last comment. "The uncle. Jake."

"Isn't he old?" I ask, wrinkling my nose.

"Sophisticated," she holds up a finger. "The patriarch."

"So really entrenched in being a crazy criminal?" I flip my hair over my shoulder as the car stops next to us, the driver getting out to open the door for us to climb in the back seat.

Jess goes first, sliding across the leather bench seat. I climb in after, my movements slower, as I sit next to my sister. "I don't understand you sometimes."

"I know." Jess would love to marry into one of the other families that make up Vegas's underworld. She doesn't seem to have a problem with the crime. All she cares about, as far as I can tell, is the lifestyle.

Then again, I'm sensitive on the topic of this lifestyle.

But I need one ally, so I don't say anymore as the car starts down the drive. And I don't want to hurt her either. I wish I could be more content sometimes. More trusting. Maybe I would have been if I hadn't learned the truth and my father hadn't turned on me in the cruelest way possible.

Silence settles for a few minutes, but my sister is never quiet for long. "You know that Russian, Mickael, that I met last week?"

"Yeah?"

"We've got another date," she whispers so the driver doesn't hear.

"How do you do it?" I ask, my eyes growing wide. "How do you get out of the house?" Because, honestly, I really want to know. This is precisely what I need Jess's help for. She is so much better at skirting around the rules than I am.

She leans in really close, whispering in my ear. "One of the guards lets me out when the cameras are turned away."

"How?" I mouth, meaning, how do you get him to do it?

She knows exactly what I'm talking about. "I blow him on the regular," she answers so softly I barely hear her. Which is why she starts pressing her tongue against her cheek, pushing the skin out to mimic a blowjob. It's on the side of her face the driver can't see, but my gaze still darts to him.

Our father, if you want to call him that, has a strict no-dating policy for both me and Jess. Though, he's way more casual with her than he is with me.

Everyone thinks it's because she's older. Or because I'm considered the beauty. And his favorite. But I know the truth.

One night when my father was fall-down drunk, he told me that he's made some arranged match for me. Barbaric.

But basically, he's planning to sell me to some distant Italian relative in marriage. Not only will he get a giant infusion of cash to save his failing business, but I will live on the other side of the Atlantic.

Basically, a whole country and an entire ocean away. For him, it's a win-win.

And I'd be out from under his power and his fists.

But I'd be some guy's trophy wife who is the same kind of criminal my dad is. No thanks.

I have no idea when this is happening, but considering that the Diamond is about to be seized by the Kincaids, I'm guessing it's very soon.

We pull into the casino, our friends waiting just outside the doors, already looking wilted in the sun.

The Vegas heat hits me full in the face and we all rush into the dark air conditioning of the lobby at the Diamond.

I hate this place.

It's all flashing lights and perfumed air that barely covers the smell of cigarette smoke.

The other girls make a beeline for the bar, ready to start drinking, and I follow behind, taking a seat at the bar with them in the last chair available.

I'm not much of a drinker and the bartender knows, pouring me a sparkling water with a lime so that it looks like a real drink. He gives me a wink to let me know this is our secret.

With a nod in return, I take a sip, settling in to listen to the ladies talk about who they're dating and who they really want to be dating, when the hair on the back of my neck stands at attention.

I turn, sweeping my gaze over the restaurant, searching for the cause.

My gaze locks with a man half hidden in the shadows. I can only see half his face, but that half makes me gasp. The piercing stare of his eyes make a jolt of electricity zing down my body.

Am I scared or excited?

It's not just that he's handsome. He is. But something in that stare is…dangerous.

I still, my fingers gripping the back of my chair as my lips open and close. What am I even trying to say? He won't hear whatever it is, he's on the other side of a crowded room.

"Hello, gorgeous," a different man says just to my right. His accent is posh and British. And then he steps in front of me, breaking the spell between me and the predator in the shadows.

I blink a few times, trying to adjust my eyes. As I take this new guy in, my brow furrows. He looks more like a Ken doll than any man I've ever seen.

I frown, just a little, weirdly irritated by the interruption. And I already know I'm not interested in this Brit. Even if I could date, his kind of classic good looks don't do it for me. Despite my complete lack of experience, I've already figured out I like dark with a healthy side of danger. This guy is all sunshine and rainbows. No thanks.

"Oh my God," Jess squeals next to me. "You're Gris Smith."

"At your service," he gives a little bow, his hands folding, one in front of his stomach and the other behind his back, like he's bowing for a king.

I automatically paste a polite smile on my face, trained since birth to be well-mannered, but as Jess makes gooey eyes at the Ken doll, I realize this might be my chance…

I need Jess's support to sneak out. And if there is one thing she'd support, it's me dating a guy like this.

Because he is part of the British invasion here in Vegas. They are buying up casinos and aligning with the Kincaids to make themselves even more powerful.

If my father can't pay the note on the Diamond, they are first in line to buy the place. I quickly reset my mouth into a softer smile. "Nice to meet you, Gris."

"I'm Jess," my sister volunteers. "And this is Nia."

"Nia," he repeats, cocking one of his perfectly arched brows. "A beautiful name for a beautiful woman."

It takes everything in me not to gnash my teeth. How corny. But I give him an even brighter smile instead. "Thank you."

"May I join you ladies?" he says, his hand resting on the back of the chair right next to mine.

I cock my head. I know I'm attractive, but this guy likely dates super models and I am not that. I may have been trained to be the perfect lady but inside, I've got a brain, a decent one. Which is why, I start quickly doing some math. I've got way more curves than the average Vegas stick figure. In other words, I'm no Barbie. Why did he seek me out? Intel? An in with my father?

Either way, if he's hoping to use me, I have every intention of using him right back.

He makes polite conversation for twenty minutes before he leans over and whispers in my ear. "Any chance I can get your number, beautiful?"

I do my best to bat my eyelashes, knowing I likely look ridiculous. But I take his phone, typing in my digits.

Jess is leaning over me, her cleavage on display as she gushes. "You know, we come here this time every week."

He cocks that brow again. "Really? So if I were to come here next week with some friends, we could all make a night of it?"

I nod, genuinely enthusiastic this time. A group date is perfect. I can hang all over him without too much worry, and then I'll convince Jess to help me sneak out for a real date.

She'll agree.

But I have no intention of actually going out with him.

No. That's my moment, and I'm going to use it to leave Vegas and never return.

I'm running away. And Gris Smith is my ticket out.

CHAPTER TWO

JAKE

I FOLD my hands sitting forward in my seat as the bride, Kim Evingston, makes her way down the aisle toward my nephew, Leo Kincaid.

Not that I recognize him. I mean, he looks mostly the same. Bulging muscles, large frame, big white-teeth smile.

Only everything else is different.

Leo normally carries this edge of anger…it rolls off him in waves, lashing out at everyone and everything he passes.

But just like that…the edge is gone.

In its place, is a wide-open, joyous smile as Leo extends his hand to the woman he's marrying.

His eyes are light and filled with…joy, as he bounces on the balls of his feet.

Leo is fucking bouncing.

I frown, trying to decide what I think about all of this. We're in the midst of a war and one of our fiercest soldiers is grinning and bouncing.

But beyond that, I can't deny that I'm happy for him.

Kim is pregnant with his baby, not that she's showing at all. As a dancer, she's still as slender as ever.

She reaches him and he pulls her into his arms, kissing her long and hard.

"Ahem," the Justice of the Peace clears her throat. "The kissing is supposed to happen at the end of the ceremony."

Leo's grin only widens. "Don't worry. There will be plenty of kissing then too."

The small crowd laughs.

Next to me is Luke, my nephew, Leo's cousin. He's got the same thick muscles and normally surly disposition that Leo's got.

He's smiling as he watches. "You ever see Leo happy like this?"

"Never." Which isn't totally true. Before the Italian Mafia killed my brother, Leo's father, Leo was happy a lot.

And somehow, Kim has brought him back to that man. It might almost make a crusty old-school asshole like myself believe in love.

Nah.

That's for other people who can afford it. And I don't mean money. Financially, I can afford whatever I want. Kincaid Enterprises is worth billions and as one of five Kincaid men, I'm an equal-share owner.

I have always been tougher, meaner than my nephews. I grew up with an old school father who was fond of using the whip and he had no trouble bringing me into the business when our family was dirty.

Not like it is now.

Mason, my oldest nephew, makes our money nice and legal. I got to hand it to him, he's done a good job.

But even now, even with Mason, we skirt on the edge of darkness. Darkness, I've always been afraid I might fall into. Like I said, I grew up different than the boys.

They need my help now. There are a few dirty jobs left, and one of them is getting revenge on Toni Carcetti. The man who killed my brother.

I know I can do what they can't, which is why I'm going to help.

Leo came up with the plan to get the job done before he went completely soft.

But now it's on me to see it through. Because anyone who sees the way Leo's holding Kim in his arms as he says his vows, they know…

Leo isn't the man for this job.

"I promise to love, honor, and cherish until death do us part." His deep voice echoes over the backyard of their new home.

A mansion in the swankiest district in Vegas, the pool sparkles in the morning sun.

Across the aisle, Kim's mom sits in a chair, Kim's roommates dabbing at their eyes.

One of them, a leggy brunette, makes eyes at me across the way. I think her name is Kendall or something.

I turn away with a barely covered snort.

I don't get mushy enough at weddings to fuck some chick because I caught some feelings.

I don't have feelings. At least not those. I've never been in love and as I'm pushing thirty-five, I think I'm a pretty baked cake. Which means, I'm not changing now, and love isn't finding me.

But I am craving more stability. Or maybe just change. Perhaps I'm tired of this life but whatever the reason, after this job is done, I'm getting out. They can buy my shares and let me start a security business of my own, away from Vegas and all the dirt.

The girl bats her eyes again, and I give her a longer appraisal. I could be sold on the idea of taking advantage of this moment and screwing one of the women here who's got bride envy.

Except, I'm smart enough to know that messing with one of Kim's friends is a choice that is likely to bite me in the ass.

And I can get tail anytime I want.

So, I sit back in my seat, listening to Kim repeat her vows, Leo grinning like a complete fool as she says them.

Christ.

He's making me a little nauseous.

I could argue that he's only marrying her because he got her pregnant. That's an old-school reason to get hitched. But I know it isn't true. Leo is in love.

He already bought a crib, even though Kim isn't due for months, and earlier this week, he invited us over to assemble it.

I'm a cigar-smoking former gangster. I don't assemble baby gear.

I drank scotch and sat in the nursing glider, because, honestly, those chairs are comfortable.

Might get one.

Has a foot stool that glides too.

Anyway, we set around with tiny stupid Allen wrenches and discussed how we were going to bring down the head of the Italian mafia here in Vegas. Not two activities you'd expect to go together.

Then again, considering the first part of this plan Leo has concocted, it's probably fitting.

I'd sipped my scotch and rocked in the glider as I watched Leo hunched on the floor.

Behind him were boxes of vibrating chairs, which are an interesting idea, and exersaucers, complete bullshit if you ask me. And I'd asked the question one last time. "You're sure she's a witness in the murder?"

"If Melissa was telling the truth, then yes." Melissa is Leo's former club manager and a backstabbing bitch, so her information is suspect in my book.

"And what if she's lying?"

"Either way, Nia is his favorite. Taking her will be your leverage to get him to confess."

I grimace even remembering the next part of my plan, my attention focusing back on the ceremony in front of me.

I've been to a few weddings.

None of them have ever been like this. There are only about fifteen guests here, our family, Kim's mom and roommates, and a few business associates. It's intimate and personal and it reminds me that marriage has the potential to be beautiful. Not a thought that is helpful today.

"I now pronounce you man and wife. You may kiss your bride."

"Finally," Leo roars and then pulls Kim tightly against him, kissing her with a whole lot of tongue.

Luke catcalls from next to me, and I give him a withering glare. Sometimes I've got to teach these boys how it's done.

Kim and Leo come back down the aisle, and we all rise, clapping for the new couple.

I have to hold back a sigh, enthusiasm is not in my emotional repertoire.

But I do smile as they reach the end of the aisle, and Leo picks up his new bride, not stopping to greet guests. Instead, he just keeps walking right into the house.

Kim lets out a small cry of protest but the men around me all chuckle.

"He doesn't want to wait to have sanctioned sex," Luke says from just behind me. "I can appreciate that."

"He's an emotional guy," Roman chuckles from the next row.

I cock my eyebrows. "When you're married, does wanting to bang your wife count as emotion?"

They all laugh at that as I catch the eye of Gris Smith, an Englishman who is part of another major family in Vegas. They call themselves the Dukes and we've made a deal with them that if they can help us out with this plan, they'll be able to acquire some choice Vegas real estate when the Italians are forced to sell it.

Gris jerks his head toward the side yard and then starts walking.

I follow, my gut clenching with dread. If he wants to talk, that means we're moving to the next phase of the plan.

We disappear around the house, leaving the rest of the guests behind. "Gris," I give him a nod. "News?"

"It will be tonight," he says with a quick dip of chin.

"Tonight?" A bit of regret lances through me. We've gone through great pains to make all this happen, but there is a part of me that hates this plan. I might be a gangster, but I don't hurt women. Doubly true for beautiful women and Nia Carcetti is most definitely one of those.

Nia is Toni Carcetti's youngest daughter, and the apple of his eye.

Gris Smith approached her at the Italian's casino and secured a date. The man is so handsome, he looks fake. And the Dukes are still relatively unknown in Vegas, which means Gris was able to fly under the radar with Nia.

He took Nia out on a group date, and then another. A few of his friends, a few of hers. Perfect gentleman both times. Toni keeps his daughters on very tight leashes. They aren't allowed to date.

But Gris, slick fuck that he is, has convinced Nia to sneak out. Tonight.

That's where I come in.

Gris hands me a set of keys with an H emblem. "A Honda?" I grumble, holding out the keys like they smell bad.

"Uber drivers don't do pick-ups in Maserati's." He slaps my shoulder. "You're going to love the Accord. Roomie interior."

I snort.

"I've had it redesigned like a cop car. No way to open the back doors from the inside. Once she's in…she's in."

From inside the house, a loud banging sound interrupts our meeting. We both look up, knowing that Leo is screwing his wife against the wall.

"He's got some serious thrusting power," Gris says appreciatively, even as the chorus of Kim's cries joins the banging.

"Kim certainly thinks so," I answer back.

Gris covers his smile with his hand. "Right. So, I'll text you as soon as I tell her that I can't pick her up because I'm running late and that I'm sending an Uber."

That's me. I'm the Uber. Only I'm not taking her to her date.

I'm taking her to a place in the desert and then I'm going to convince her to betray her father by any means necessary. I've come armed with several tools. The biggest, or at least the most expensive, an engagement ring…

Not that I'm the marrying kind. I've no intention of doing what Leo did today. But I'll do whatever it takes to convince Nia to switch sides, change her loyalties, and if that means a fake offer of marriage. So be it.

Yeah. If you're thinking that I might lack for the charm for this, you'd be right. But I'm going to have to dig deep and find a way. Because while I may lack the charm, I've got the grit. The morally gray center that will allow me to do what I don't think my nephews could.

Deceive and ruin a potentially innocent woman.

And then I'm getting out.

But that's a problem for after. Right now, I need to focus on the task at hand. Toni Carcetti is going down, and his daughter Nia is going to help me whether she likes it or not.

CHAPTER THREE

Nia

I apply my lip gloss and give myself a final check. I've got on a cute fitted dress with tank straps and a skirt almost to the knees. It looks date worthy, but I can easily put the cardigan I've packed in my bag over it and be comfortable on a plane.

I grimace in the mirror.

Ghosting Gris isn't going to be the most fun thing I've ever done. I'm not attracted to the guy, but honestly, he's been nothing but polite.

And he hasn't mentioned my father once. It would be so much easier if he had.

I could dismiss him as an asshole.

But no, he's been a complete gentleman on our two group dates. Maybe he's gay and looking for a cover wife?

I cock my head. That might have been an interesting plan, but I've already invested in my current one.

And who knows how long a courtship like that would take and I don't have the time. Toni is planning for this other family to come visit so that I can meet the man he's planned for me to marry. Not happening.

I've bought myself a ticket to Ontario. From there, I'll pay cash to buy a small car and drive to Quebec. I don't have a license, but I convinced my cousin to give me a couple of driving lessons. Hopefully, they'll be enough.

In my bag is hair dye—I'm going brunette—and the bare essentials for toiletries and clothes.

Jess still thinks I'm going on a date so I couldn't pack too much. I did manage to stow another small bag in the bushes out back. I've got maybe three days' worth of clothes in there. I wish I could have brought more, but the bag had to be small enough to remain hidden and my purse has to appear to Jess, not like I'm running away, and more like I've finally developed a love of cosmetics.

It's believable. Most girls would develop a love of products dating a guy like Gris. Jess certainly would.

And she's the only reason I'm getting out tonight and she's the one who'll cover for me when I text her and tell her the date is going really well and I won't be home tonight.

Right on cue, she knocks on my door.

"Come in."

She opens it, looking a bit flushed in her cheeks, her eyes glassy. "You're good to head out the back. Meet Mike by the door in the kitchen."

Her blush deepens. Mike must be the guy she's blowing. Did she give him another to get me out tonight? That's way more altruistic than my sister usually behaves. I wonder what's really going on between them?

Does he know she's using him to go out with other guys? Does he care? "Thanks, Jess."

She nods. "Do me a favor and land this guy. They're going to be big players, and you'll set us both up if you do."

"Set us up?" But I'm starting to understand. She's got a vested interest.

She shrugs. "I'm not sure Dad is doing all that great. We need to find men who can sustain us."

I give a curt nod. I knew about Dad's finances, but I'm surprised she's paid enough attention to notice. Then again, it's one area she might be deeply vested. Not that I'm knocking my sister. She should understand what's about to happen to her and I sincerely hope she finds a way out before it does. Jess might be interested in being plastic but she's not a bad person. In fact, no one has done more for me. I wish I could tell her the truth. I'm so tired of it being between us.

I wish I could be different, a real sister instead of this frozen statue.

"Thanks for doing this, Jess. I really appreciate it."

She steps into the room. "You do it for me all the time. It's the least I can do. Besides," her gaze slides away, "I don't know what guy Dad's picked for you in Italy, but I know he won't be as hot as Gris."

She knows about that too? I reach for her hand, giving it a squeeze. I'd like to say more, tell her I love her, but I can't make the words come out.

I push up from my chair and cross to give her a hug. She hugs me back, squeezing me tight. "Go get him and get out of here. And I mean tonight and permanently."

I squeeze her one last time and then grab my bag, dashing out the door before I get confessional. Creeping my way down to the kitchen, I check every hall and doorway. Not that I need to bother.

It's a Saturday night and the house is empty. The guards on site are tasked with keeping us safe and keeping us locked away. Mike must not realize what my dad is capable of to be helping us like this. He prizes loyalty above all else.

Not that he's loyal to anyone. Not even family.

I make my way down the kitchen, the back door open. It's never open.

Stepping outside, I find a good-looking guard I'd never noticed before leaning against the house, smoking a cigarette, looking very relaxed.

I say a silent thank you to Jess as he points toward a door by the back gate. "It's unlocked. The cameras swing back around in five so you better hurry."

With a nod, I start across the lawn, hefting my bag higher on my shoulder. It's that moment my phone chimes.

I don't look, dashing across the grass to where my suitcase is stashed. Lifting it with my other hand, I sprint to the emergency door that is partially hidden by some bushes. I've seen the door a thousand times, so I don't have to hunt.

Twisting the knob, I'm almost surprised when it's actually unlocked. Tugging, it swings open, and I step out onto the back street behind our property.

I can't believe I'm here. Outside the walls with no guard and no father... Drawing in a deep gulp of air, I close my eyes for a split second. I'm going to be free...

Lifting my phone, I check the text, cursing under my breath. It's Gris. He's going to be late...

What the hell am I supposed to do?

But then I see another message come through.

Got you an Uber. I'll meet you at the restaurant.

Always a gentleman. I could give Gris that.

Awesome. Thanks. Tell the driver to meet me on Elm St.

Three dots appear again. *Will do. He'll be there in five. Black Honda Accord.*

I let out a long breath. Five. I can handle five.

. . .

THE TRUTH IS I was a bubbly, earnest kid, but being the victim of Toni's tyranny has changed me, hardened me, made me tougher. But underneath that…

I start to pace, wondering if I should start walking. Get away from the house?

But just as my feet get so antsy I can't stay still another second, a black car pulls down the street. It only takes a second for me to identify the H emblem on the front and I wilt with relief.

This is my Uber.

The car stops next to me. If the driver thinks it's strange he's not meeting me by the front door, he doesn't say. "Antonia?" Under normal circumstances, I might wonder why the guy is still wearing sunglasses in the dark, but I'm just relieved he's here. And I've heard enough stories about Uber drivers to know they can be weird.

I've never used one before, because Toni has us driven by the family driver everywhere, but I play it cool.

"That's me," I chirp and then make a dart for the back door, sliding into the car and pulling the door shut. "You're quick."

"I aim to please," he says, as he shifts the car in drive and pulls away. "Acapulco's?"

I shake my head to say *no,* already pulling out my phone to check my flight info. The Uber makes this so much quicker and easier. I don't have to go through the motions of starting the date with Gris, of leaving halfway through the meal. "Change of plans. I'd like to go to the airport."

"The airport?" he asks, his deep voice tensing in a way I didn't expect.

"Is that a problem?" Did Gris prepay or something? I can always have this guy drive me to the restaurant and then catch a cab from there. What I don't need is complications, and I've got money if I have to pay for a ride myself.

I never spend my allowance, and so I've several thousand dollars in travelling cash.

"No problem," he answers, clearing his throat.

"Oh good. I was worried."

"It's just not many guys get an Uber for their date to have her go to the airport instead." He puts on the blinker and turns left toward the highway.

I slide back in my seat and pull out my phone again. Relief washes through me when my flight information pops up as on time.

But something is tickling the back of my brain. I raise my head again. This guy is way too up in my business. How does he even know it's a date?

When I note his gaze is back on the road, silence settling again, I don't ask. Why bother? I'm probably just being paranoid, considering my plan. Lifting my phone, I start doing the mobile check-in for my flight. I wish I could have packed more clothes.

I start to hum as I click buttons, relief and excitement, turning my humming into a soft song. If I have one place that still makes me feel, it's singing.

"You've got a great voice," the driver says, making me stop singing, my lips pressing together. But I appreciate the compliment.

"Thanks." I'm hoping to use my voice to make some under-the-table cash while I'm hiding out in Canada.

I know it's a little high-profile, but it's also my best chance of working a little here and there without documentation. Paid in cash.

I had to use my regular passport to enter Canada, which I think means my father can track me.

At least I've got a fake Canadian ID to buy the car.

I pull up marketplace and type in Ontario, looking for a car I might be able to buy.

"Where you headed?"

Irritation makes me sit up as my eyes flick back up and catch his gaze in the mirror. At least I think I catch it. His sunglasses are still on.

But I can see the cut of his jaw and the stubble that does nothing to hide that it's square and deliciously masculine, his mouth full and sexy as hell with his half smile.

I blink away these thoughts. Why am I lusting after the weird Uber driver who keeps interrupting me? I don't lust. I'd never give another man that kind of power over me. "Boston," I say automatically, returning to my phone.

"What's in Boston?"

"My date."

"Ah," he answers, pulling onto the highway. Relieved to finally have stumped him, I go back to my phone.

There is a Honda Civic dirt-cheap for sale right outside Ontario proper. "How do you like the Accord?"

"Surprisingly roomy," he answers with a half grin in the mirror. The smile makes my stomach do funny flips.

I look away, my cheeks heating. "I guess I was wondering more about reliability or drivability. Is it easy to drive?"

"Both are excellent," he answers, the car gliding smoothly along the highway. "Very easy driving."

"Thanks." I give a nod and then fire off a message to the seller, asking to meet tomorrow. The sooner I start on my trip east across Canada, the better off I'll be.

Letting out a long breath, I wonder how long it will take the guy to respond to my request to see the car, when I see the airport sign up ahead.

My shoulders unwind. Every successful step puts a bit more distance between me and Toni Carcetti.

For a moment my eyes flutter closed. I don't care how difficult freedom is, it'll be better than the prison in which I've been living.

But the moment my eyes open, my chin jerks back in surprise. "Hey. You just drove by the airport exit."

"Did I?" he says, not meeting my gaze in the rearview. "I'll turn around at the next exit."

I give the barest nod, my fingers clenching around my phone. I've got tons of time. I planned a whole hour and a half to first meet and then lose Gris on our date. Which means this is no big deal. But every hiccup makes me nervous.

Speaking of...I'm surprised Gris hasn't texted. I should have been at the restaurant by now and so should he.

But maybe if he's still running late, it's a blessing.

The next exit comes up, but the car doesn't decelerate, nor do we move from the middle lane, to the right.

"I thought you were going to turn around?" I say, real panic beginning to rise in my chest. Why didn't we exit the highway?

He doesn't look at me this time, nor does he answer as we glide past the exit. "Hey," I say again, my voice getting louder, sharper. "I really need you—"

"Nia."

The name, my name, cuts me right to the bone. He called me Antonia when he first picked me up. I'm sure of it. Why would the Uber driver know my nickname?

And then he pulls his sunglasses down, his eyes meeting mine.

I recognize them instantly. He was at the Diamond the night I met Gris.

Even in the dark, illuminated only by the headlights of oncoming traffic, this close, I can see they are a piercing gray color, the intensity of them stealing my breath. "You."

"You know who I am?"

"I know you were at the Diamond a few weeks back."

"I was."

The same night I met Gris. Suddenly, the reason Gris isn't worried I'm late is completely clear.

He was a set-up all along. I knew that guy was too good to be true. Not that I can worry about him right now. My hand claws at my throat as I freeze for a moment. What do I do?

I automatically reach for a door handle, though I don't know where I think I'm going with the car cruising down the highway at eighty miles an hour.

But shock hits me when I realize there isn't a latch to open the door. I blink at the empty mechanism, trying to process why the tab would be missing, my heart racing in my chest.

"Nia." The driver says again. "I'm going to need you to give me your phone."

"No," I whisper, clutching the device tighter. I have to call my father. I hate Toni Carcetti, but I know he'll come for me.

Hitting the screen, I fumble to type in the code, press the buttons that will make this all better.

That's when the driver's right hand appears on the back of the passenger's seat, a small pistol resting casually in his grip. "The phone, Nia. Now."

I've got to hand it to him, the threat, casually delivered is immediately effective. But as I lift my sweating hand up, the phone falls from my grip, bouncing, still lit, onto the floor and then under his seat.

I let out a strangled gasp, staring at where it disappeared. How bad was that…is he going to… "It went under the seat," I cry, feeling the fear swelling inside me. I'm pretty good at controlling it most times, but this is so unexpected and crazy. I just…

"Hey," he says, and he doesn't sound upset. In fact, it's soft, soothing. "Just relax and everything will be fine."

My gaze snaps back to his in the mirror. "Fine? You're kidnapping me."

"Don't think of it like that," he answers smoothly. With the sunglasses off, I can see he's as handsome and as sinister as I imagined that night at the Diamond. Not that I should be taking note of that detail.

This guy's a pyscho.

I wrap my arms around myself, barely holding back a sob. I wanted to get away, but in this moment, I'd do nearly anything to be safely tucked back in my room, under the care of Toni Carcetti.

CHAPTER FOUR

Nia

I sink down lower in my seat, wondering what sort of fresh hell I've landed myself in now. What is this man going to do to me?

I suddenly realize that I'm breathing so heavily, I'm beginning to hyperventilate. "What do you want with me? Why am I here? Are you going to hurt me?"

The car slows as he lets off the gas. "No."

He didn't have to answer but I barely acknowledge that as I try to calm my racing heart. I've suffered abuse before and fists I can take. But other types of assault make my stomach pitch. "I'd rather you just killed me than…." The words are out before I can hold them back, but I bite back the second half of that sentence, not wanting to say what I'm worried he'll do out loud.

"Nia," he says my name like my words have pained him. Him. Some niggle of anger helps me to gain control. Why should my death hurt him? I'm the one who's been forced against my will. Something, I guess I'm used to. Thanks to Toni.

"My father will come for me."

"I know." His voice is so calm and so assured that my mouth drops open. Is that the plan? Am I bait?

"What will you do with me while we wait?" The fear is sliding back in, my limbs begin to shake as he slows the car down, pulling over to the side.

Casually, he reaches under his seat and then pulls up my phone. With a quick strike using the butt of the gun, he smashes the device, then rips it apart. In a final move, he tosses it out the window.

And then we're off again.

I look back out the window, like the phone was my final lifeline. Maybe it was.

"To answer your question, I'm not going to do anything with you."

I blink, turning back to him. "What do you mean?"

"What I said. We're going to spend some time getting to know each other. That's it."

I shake my head. That doesn't sound all that reassuring. That's the kind of creepy thing some rapist would say to cover his real meaning.

"It really helps that you ditched Gris tonight. At least I know you're not pining for that Brit."

Does he realize he's given something away? I suspected Gris was involved, but now it's been confirmed, I know exactly who to tell my father to kill. Gris Smith is at the top of the list. Fucker.

And Toni will. If there is one thing I know about my father, he's a killer.

"I'm Jake Kincaid, by the way. Pleased to meet you."

I shake my head, trying to put this together. My kidnapper is just giving me his identity? He must be planning to kill me. "Are you going to rape me first? Because the term 'getting to know each other' sounds like code."

The car jerks, Jake's eyes meeting mine in the mirror. "I would never—"

I shake my head, cutting off his words. "Why would I believe you?"

His mouth tightens, pressing into a thin line. "Listen very closely. I am not going to hurt you. Unlike your father, I have never hurt a woman in my life."

I swallow, because it's kind of refreshing to speak the truth about the man I have to pretend to love every day. Silver lining? Maybe. "You know that about him, do you?"

"I know a lot of terrible things about him."

My shoulders wilt as I look down in my lap. I had no idea I needed to hear someone say that so badly. "He's a monster."

"Yes. He is." I needed to hear someone say that too. Shit. How does this guy know what my heart has been pining for?

I shake my head, tears stinging my eyes. I never cry. Not anymore. And I can't afford to fall into the guy who has just stolen me. "So what are you here for? What am I here for?"

"We can help each other." He gets off at the next exit and for a moment, I think we might stop. Maybe I can get away…

But he only reverses direction, heading the opposite way down the highway.

Which makes sense. If anyone tracked my phone, we'd want to change direction. And that's the moment I realize I am in way over my head.

He's got a plan and it's methodical, and he isn't even trying to hide his identity, which means he's got really good reasons for giving me his name. It wasn't a mistake. He wanted me to know it.

My eyes flutter closed again, and I sink down until I'm lying on the back seat. I don't cry, at least not audibly. I've got iron control over my emotions. I just focus on drawing the next breath.

"You good, sweetheart?" He sounds…concerned.

I don't answer. Will my lack of cooperation make him stop the car? Hurt me? I don't know. But I keep my lips clamped shut.

"Nia." His voice holds a command I don't ignore this time. I intimately understand the danger of ignoring a man who has power over you.

"If you wanted to help me, you'd drop me at the airport." The words are whispered into the seat, but he seems to hear them anyway.

"And why were you going to the airport?"

"To take a flight."

"Where? Why?"

"Why am I in this car?" I don't meet his eyes. They scare me. Instead, I keep mine closed, my face pressed into the upholstery that smells like new car.

"I told you, we're going to help each other."

"How are you helping me?" I breathe through my nose, trying to keep my head. I'll die silent before I allow him to use me to hurt my family. I may not love Toni but there are people who should be protected. My sister's face fills my thoughts.

"Where were you going? You snuck out for a date. Why go to the airport?" I let out a breath and lift my head, trying to figure out what he wants.

My stomach pitches with the movement. "I think I might be sick."

Something cool touches my hand and I snap my eyes open to see a bucket in front of my face. He even thought to bring a vomit bucket.

I take the plastic container and hold it below my face. The car hums along and I realize that I should be watching where we're going. Paying attention.

But my head is pounding, and my stomach is rolling. It's been silent for a few minutes when Jake speaks again. "See, I think that you were running away."

I don't open my eyes. I'm still trying to control my stomach. "Maybe I'm just wild."

He gives a small laugh. "You socialize once a week at the same place at the same time. Other than that, you're rarely seen socially, except with your father. That's your version of wild?"

My father…

It's not lost on me this man knows my whereabouts, my habits. Should that make me feel better? This is all very methodical. Planned. Does that make him more or less likely to hurt me? "I don't…"

"See, I think I was right, and you were running away from Toni."

I can barely focus as I sink my face deeper in the bucket. "What if I was?"

"Well…in that case, you can think of this as me helping you."

My eyes pop open and I sit up, intent upon telling him where he can stick his help. But my stomach pitches again, this time not to be tamed, and I'm grabbing the bucket as the contents of my afternoon snack land in the plastic container.

"Shit," he says as he pulls the car over. I retch until there is nothing left and I'm panting as my heartrate slowly comes back down. Silently, he reaches back. "Give me the bucket."

I hand it over the seat, no fight in me, and he opens his door, dumping the contents on the side of the highway.

What weird universe am I living in right now? Part of me wonders if this is my moment to escape, but my head is swimming, my body weak, and honestly, I'm never getting into the front seat, past him, and out the door. I need to pick a better moment.

Instead, I wilt back into the bench seat, wrapping my arms around myself. I don't even realize I'm shivering until he shrugs of his jacket, a buttery leather, and drapes it over my torso.

That calms something inside me. If rape and torture were his game, would he be placing clothing over me to keep me warm?

I pull the jacket tighter about my body when the scent of it hits my nose. It's spicy and masculine with a touch of cigar scent laced through it. It smells amazing. I want to curl into that scent.

Weird, since the man who carries it is my kidnapper. "What did you say your name was?"

"Jake."

Jake. Jake is not one of Mason's brothers. I know their names. Leonard. Roman. Jake is the…uncle. "How come you told me your name?"

"I'm not here to hurt you, Nia. Like I said, I want us to help each other."

"And the gun?"

His eyes meet mine in the rearview again. The same shock runs through me, but I'm not so scared this time, more curious. Interested. And confused. How does he think I might help him? "Just a way to make sure we had enough time to make sure we really talked."

The questions swirling in my thoughts help to add a bit of rigidity to my muscles. "How can you help me?"

"If you wanted to run away, disappear, then I've done you a large favor. Because you just left Vegas without a trace."

"That's supposed to comfort me? That no one can find me and I'm with a strange man who stole me?"

He quirks a half grin, making him even more handsome. Mysterious. "I'm not going to hurt you. Not one hair on your pretty head. I promise you that."

I shake my head. He sounds serious but I don't know how I could possibly trust these words. "Why am I here then?"

"In tomorrow's papers, there is going to be an announcement."

Is he ignoring my question? "Oh yeah. What's that?"

"The announcement? That you and I are engaged."

My mouth drops open. "What?" I can't even make sense of the words. Why would he print that…my family will think…

"See. If anything happens to you, I'm suspect number one. It's your insurance I won't hurt you."

But the ramifications of it send a shiver down my spine. My father won't think I've been kidnapped. He'll think I ran away from the shit wedding he's planned for me. Which I was…but worse, they'll all think that I betrayed them and then Toni's going to… "I really am the bait to tempt Toni," I mutter.

"Don't think of it like that." We slip through the desert, the dark of the night more comforting than I thought it would be.

"So just to be clear. People, my family, are going to think that you and I eloped?"

"That's right, Mrs. Kincaid."

"You're even crazier than I thought." I really am going to need to escape because if my family manages to get me back, I'll have to pray that the Italian boss is very enamored with me. He'll be my only hope of living to see Christmas.

He chuckles at that. "And you're funnier than I thought."

I let out a rush of air. Why is he so calm? He's committing a major crime and…he's probably used to that. My father is. Does he know what he's doomed me to? I didn't want to stay in Vegas before, now there is no choice at all.

"You have to know that I'm not marrying you."

"Technically, I said we got engaged. Not that we married. Just so we're clear."

"Crystal. Why would I think you would make good on a public offer?" My lip curls. Much of my fear is gone, replaced with a reckless need to lash out. Maybe he'll kill me quickly in a fit of rage and this will all be over. I'm so tired…

"Is that a specific insult to me?" He doesn't sound like he's gone into a rage. In fact, curiosity laces his deep baritone. Maybe even amusement.

"Nope. I just meant you're all part of the same crooked beast that runs Vegas's filthy businesses."

"My family rarely breaks laws. But your father has attacked both of the women we protect and—"

"So I'm up for grabs then? It's justified to hurt me?"

"I'm not hurting you," he says, his eyes level. "I would never hurt you. But after your father is locked away and spending his life in prison, you can make the choice where you want to go. What you want to do."

I stare at him, my mouth hanging open. He thinks I could just go back to my family after this? Either he doesn't understand anything, he's lying, or he really is off his rocker…

CHAPTER FIVE

NIA

WE DRIVE for at least three hours, the last half hour on some tiny desert road. It has to be midnight when the car finally stops in front of a small house in the middle of nowhere.

We haven't talked for a few hours. I watched where we drove, but we changed highways at least a dozen times.

My head is aching and with the darkness preventing me from seeing landmarks, I'm not sure I could ever make my way back.

Jake Kincaid is so many steps ahead of me, it makes my head spin.

I missed my flight an hour ago and I've no phone to text Jess. Will she cover for me anyway?

Or is Toni learning that I'm gone?

Will he find me out in the desert? My phone is by the airport. If it gets tracked to there…

Everyone will assume I boarded a plane.

And the announcement will hit the papers. The world will think I'm engaged. That I eloped with Jake?

No one is coming here to look…

Should I be relieved or scared out of my mind? I shake my head, with no idea what to even feel.

Jake gets out of the car and opens my door. I stare at him as he reaches a hand in to help me out.

We are not touching…

I cross my arms and glare. "I don't need your hand."

He only reaches it further into the car. "Sorry, sweetheart, but I can't have you running."

"Run where?" I snort, as I continue to sit. "I've lived around Vegas long enough to understand the dangers of the desert."

Slowly, he lowers his hand and takes a step back. I inch toward the open door, watching him as I swing one foot out of the car, then the other.

He takes another step back, allowing me to push off the seat. The cool night air hits my face and I draw in a deep breath.

Jake grabs my bags and then points toward the house. "This way."

He doesn't lead the way, though, waiting for me and walking next to me as he carries my bags.

We even look like a couple as he pulls out a key, opening the door and inviting me inside as he holds my stuff.

"You didn't bring a suitcase?" I ask, stepping into the small, but beautiful, interior. A kitchen is to the left, a small island doubling as a table. It has clean, modern lines but with natural-wood finishes that make it feel so cozy. An overstuffed couch and chairs sit to the right, overlooking large windows that face out into the darkness.

"I've already moved in," he answers, closing the door behind us, a lock clicking into place. How did it close? I should be tracking the details but I'm so tired and my head is throbbing.

I should be planning my escape but I'm exhausted and I don't have a clue how. My eyes sweep over the room again, noting a small hall with three doors. One on the end, and two facing each other. Two bedrooms and a bath?

When was the last time that I peed?

He starts toward the doors, entering the room on the left, still carrying my bags.

It takes a second but then I realize...I'm alone.

I have no idea how long I've got but I spin back to the door. I heard it lock but I try the handle anyway.

It doesn't budge.

With a quick breath, I turn back and that's when I notice the block of knives on the counter.

Racing into the kitchen, I pull one from the block. Smaller, but with a sinister looking blade, I shove on my cardigan and push the blade up my sleeve.

I take the two steps out of the small space just as he reappears from the bedroom.

I have this moment where I'm trying to decide. What do I do with the knife? Do I use it now? Wait?

He stops three feet away from me, his eyes narrowing. "Nia. You all right?"

"I..." I swallow down a lump. "I need to use the bathroom."

He points at the center door behind him, and I start toward it. I'm not sure what I'm hoping to accomplish, but I'm tired and I need a moment to think it through.

I brush past him, quickly entering the room and close the door. I really do need to go pee, and I pull down my panties and sit. The bathroom is as nicely appointed as the rest of the place. It really would be a lovely house to stay in if not for the whole "held against my will" part.

Pulling the knife from my sleeve, I hold it in my hand. *Think, Nia. What are you doing?* I could trust him. He says he wants to help me. I snort at the ridiculousness.

The blade catches the light as I stare. I could kill him.

I let out a long breath of air, my eyes closing. I'm holding the handle in my grip. Am I a killer?

The only person I've ever tried to hurt is myself...

I was fourteen, my mom had been dead for a year. I knew the truth about Toni, and I'd seen his love for me turn to hate.

I thought it might be better if I just...

"Are you hungry? You missed dinner." Jake calls from the kitchen.

My knuckles are white on the blade, my breath coming out in short gasps. I don't answer.

He doesn't ask again.

A beat goes by. Two. And I stare at the knife, wondering if I'm better or worse off if I just end it here. I had that same thought in the car. What am I fighting for? Life is closing in on all sides…

Suddenly, the door flies open…

Jake stands in the doorway for a split second, his eyes filled with lightning as a growl rumbles from his chest.

I'm still on the toilet, my dress up to my waist, panties around my knees as I stare up at him, my mouth surely open and my eyes wide.

In a second, he's across the bathroom, his hand wrapping tight around my wrist, the knife still in my hand. "What are you doing?" he growls.

"I…" A lump forms in my throat. Is it crazy that I feel ashamed? For a second I want to explain. I wasn't going to hurt myself…probably. I was contemplating hurting him first. But why should I offer him an explanation?

He's the one who stole me. Why should I believe him when he says he's not going to hurt me?

He puts a little more pressure on my wrist until I cry out and loosen my grip on the handle.

He takes the instrument from my hand, tossing it out of the bathroom and down the hall. I watch it sail through the air, refusing to think about what is going to happen next.

That's one of the ways you survive abuse. You don't think.

"You are not hurting yourself, Nia," he growls out. "Didn't I tell you that I was here to protect you?"

Then he leaves the bathroom, softly closing the door behind him.

I stare at the spot where he just was. Because this is not how men in my world act. They don't softly close the door when you've disobeyed. And they never mean the words when they say they'll protect you.

Something small in me cracks and I realize that I might actually want to believe him.

CHAPTER SIX

JAKE

IT TAKES everything in me not to smash a window when I stride back into the kitchen. Was she going to use that knife on herself?

My blood is pumping ice cold. With all my carefully planned scenarios, that was never one of them.

It never occurred to me that she'd be a danger to herself.

Fuck.

Was it just this morning that I sneered at Kim and Leo and declared myself immune to feelings? I'm clearly not the brightest bulb, because I did not see this coming.

I'm in over my head and she's way more fragile than I thought.

But there is no going back now.

I'm not a man who's in touch with his feelings. I do strength. I do hate. I pepper them both with sarcasm. The largest compliment any one person gets from me is something like...*you're not half bad.*

That's it.

I think back to the sound of her vomiting in the back of the car. It tore me apart that I'd scared a woman hard enough that she'd thrown up in fear. And it makes me sick to my stomach too.

Because as much as I'm not sappy, I'm also not cruel. My pops could never train that into me, as much as he tried.

And she in her fear, in her fragility, she's stripping back all my defenses. Already. Fuck. Fuck. Fuck.

I've made a mistake. Parts of this plan are just fucking mean and as much as it's meant to hurt Toni, Nia is going to be collateral damage. I know that even as I sell her safety.

Does that make me like him? Did he make me as cruel as he was? And why the fuck is that just occurring to me now?

I don't plan on hurting her myself, not like my pops would have. He'd swing his fists at any member of our family, including my mom.

I would never do that. I'd lock myself in a cell first. But I still know what happens to her after. And it isn't going to be pretty.

I thought I was fine with that. I wasn't hurting her.... I was still different. And I was doing this to protect my family. But this isn't going to end well for Nia.

Then again. Toni Carcetti would do far worse if he got his hands on one of our women. He's done worse to his own, if the rumors are true. What they say he did to his wife makes my pops look like a saint.

Is it true? That's what I'm here to find out.

I cross the room and pick up the knife. I've likely ruined the blade throwing it like that. Still, I slide the utensil back in the block and take the entire block and place my index finger over the invisible pad that unlocks one of the cabinet doors.

I let out a growl of frustration at my own stupidity. I was here, setting up the house last week. When I made myself dinner, I left the block out and never put it back.

I've used every trick in my security repertoire on this place. Fingerprint locks, cameras, digital feeds, electrified perimeter. And it's all run by a solar array I installed myself. It's apocalypse proof and what I plan to do for work when this is all done.

Sliding the block in the locked cabinet, I hear the toilet flush and then the faucet come on.

I scrub my hands down my face as I picture her with water running all down her body. Nia's beauty is another problem.

It's tempting and distracting, neither of which I can afford. I am here because no one wants revenge on her father more than me, and no man is as immune to the charms of women more than me.

It makes me ideal to coerce Nia into sharing Toni's dark secrets. The problem, however, is that she's stroking sympathies I thought long dead.

I'm going to blame the wedding. Leo looking all gooey-eyed is messing with my head.

Or perhaps I should have done this differently. Maybe I should have talked to her at the Diamond. Convinced her to run away with me instead of cutting corners.

Another rumble leaves my chest. I would have been recognized at the Diamond's bar. That's the first problem. But worse...

I would have had to charm her into leaving with me, and let's be honest...that's a stretch.

But now, she's scared in ways that are tugging on my sympathies, which is a problem I did not foresee.

How is this happening? We've been together for hours, not even days. I'm going to have to put some more steel in my spine.

Nia appears next to me, clearing her throat. "Can I get my toothbrush out of my bag? I need to brush my teeth."

I straighten up, my eyes flitting down Nia. Her long blonde hair is spilling over one shoulder, her arms wrapped around her middle, pushing her cleavage even higher and fuller while doing little to hide her stunning hourglass figure.

She makes a man ache.

Large blue eyes meet mine and then skitter away as she nips at her full lip. She looks frightened, weak, and stunning in ways that just makes me want to protect her. Christ. Why did I have to start caring now?

Her lip is trembling, and her eyes are the slightest bit watery, but her chin is high. I resist the urge to reach out and touch her.

"Of course," I answer, and she turns toward the bedroom as I follow. She was going to the airport, so I doubt there are any weapons in her bags but our little incident with the knife has me on high alert.

She unzips her small bag and pulls out a case. I'm in the doorway and I hold out my hand, opening the bag and checking the contents. Again.

I'd already looked when I brought them into the room. It's the task I was completing when she managed to smuggle the knife into the bathroom.

"How come there are two twin beds in here?" she asks as I give her the bag back, not so much as a nail clipper inside.

She's not going to like the answer. With a shrug, I start for the kitchen. "How do you feel about chicken tacos?"

"What?"

"Chicken tacos. You need to eat, and I know you were on your way to Mexican when I picked you up."

She doesn't answer as I head to the kitchen, making quick work of an easy meal. When she reappears, I'm slicing an avocado to add to the dish.

"I don't think I'm hungry," she whispers, standing on the other side of the counter.

I have a choice here. I can insist. Demand she eat the food I've provided. I'm a-hole enough to do it.

If she were one of my nephews, I'd tell her she was an idiot and then leave it. But you can't speak to ladies like that and then gain their trust. This is one of the many reasons I don't date. Women are so much more…complicated. And I don't trust myself. Never have.

But I have to try. Trust is crucial here, and I've got to start building some if I'm going to accomplish my goals. I don't think about after I've gotten what I want. "You've got to be hungry."

"I'm not—"

"I meant what I said, Nia. I'm not going to hurt you. If you let me, I'll take care of you."

I see her shoulders sink. "You should have taken my sister. She'd like nothing more than to be held in the loving…" she says the last word on a sneer, "embrace of your family."

I know Nia's sister. Unlike Nia who remains mostly out of the public eye, Jessica spends as much time as possible in it. She's like most women who fill Vegas. Thin as rails except for the fake boobs, lots of makeup, hair dye, and surgery. A carefully crafted façade that takes massive amounts of money and effort to keep up. Those women have never been my thing.

But Nia… "You think she'd want to be here with me? In the middle of the desert outside of Vegas? Would she run away?"

Nia shakes her head. "She wouldn't run away. But she'd join another family in an instant."

So Toni doesn't have the loyalty to either of his daughters. See? Conversation is already gaining me valuable information. "Something tells me that Jessica would not suit me."

Nia shrugs. "What woman suits a kidnapper?"

One corner of my mouth tilts up because I like a bit of sass. "Fine. You don't like me. But I will not hurt you and think of it this way: if you're going to outwit me, you'll need your energy." And then I push the plate closer.

I see her eyes dart to dish, her desire for the food clear. "It's safe?"

Safer than knives in the bathroom. "Sweetheart, if I wanted to hurt you, I wouldn't drive hours to then poison you with dinner."

She nods as though that makes complete sense and then she slips onto a stool, heaps some avocado on her taco, wraps it up, and takes a big bite.

I feel like I just won some major victory as I grab the other plate and take a large bite myself.

She eats the entire taco without a word and then looks up at me. "Can I make myself another?"

I sigh, realizing we need to be clearer on the arrangement. "The food is yours to eat as much as you want as often as you want. Tomorrow, I'll show you the workout space and the library."

"There's a library?" she asks, her eyes brightening like I've just told her it's Christmas. Beautiful, sassy, and smart. I shouldn't even notice.

I take my last bite of taco, and chew thoughtfully, wanting to insert a slight pause in this conversation. When I've swallowed, I watch as she eats her second taco, some of the color returning to her cheeks.

Opening another cabinet, I pull out the bourbon and pour two short glasses. "Drink?"

She hesitates. "I'm not much of a drinker."

I take one glass and wave it under my nose, inhaling. I'd like to have about five of these, but I've got to keep my wits. "A sip will help you sleep."

She looks skeptically at the glass, licking her lips like she'd like to try it.

I'm deeply invested in making certain this woman is happy and healthy while she's here. Comfort is key to the plan. "Nia. I told you… think of this as a vacation. Eat, sleep, read, relax. Drink. You are safe here and no one is going to hurt you." Silently, I add the words, *no one is going to find you either. Not until I want them to.*

CHAPTER SEVEN

Nia

After I finish the drink, I take a shower, singing as I wash the vomit from my hair, and then put on my pajamas, an old T-shirt and some running shorts, and climb into one of the twin beds.

I'm sure the room is set up with two because this is a two-bedroom for a family and the other bedroom is the master.

I hear Jake in the bathroom, and I let out a long breath.

So far, everything has been as promised. But my brain can't quite wrap around the whole situation.

Who would be able to relax? Jake is way too handsome and then there is the whole *think of your kidnapping like a vacation*. In what world does that make sense?

I come from a messed-up criminal family, and not even I think this is reasonable.

Except, I come from a family where the men hurt their women. Like all the time. It's not just my dad. My aunt is a classic case of an abused-and-battered woman, she flinches at everything.

And don't even get me started on some of my cousins. The

Vendetti twins could make any woman's skin crawl. They were torture-the-animals kind of kids.

I've got to be honest. Toni is terrible. Do I have some of those same markers as my aunt? Probably. I barely speak, I don't connect with anyone. Not even my sister.

I am currently sporting bruises on my ribs and the outside of my thighs because Toni got really drunk when he found out Mason was foreclosing on the Diamond and took his frustration out on me.

The Kincaids have been hitting Toni hard. First, they got the oldest Vendetti arrested, and then Little Anthony, Toni's second in command. Which means, Toni's been hitting me extra hard.

I'm half convinced I'd already be married but I need unmarked skin for the wedding night.

Not that Toni's broken me. Toni hasn't made me weak. If anything, I've gotten stronger. Or maybe that's the wrong word. I'm just…harder.

I think back on what Jess said. About how other families could protect us and how we'd need that. There is some sound logic there, even if I want nothing to do with this life.

And despite understanding her point, I know I don't want to get tangled up with the Kincaids. They can claim to operate on the right side of the law but kidnapping definitely falls under the creepy-as-hell category, no matter how hot they are.

As if to underscore my point, the bedroom door opens, and Jake walks into the room.

I sit up with a gasp, clutching the covers to my chest, like those are going to protect me. "Wh-wh-what are you doing?"

"Going to bed," he says as he walks between the two beds, close enough that I can smell his aftershave, and I shrink away. It's a perfectly nice scent. Delicious, even, but this is just too much.

He only turns to the other bed and pulls back the covers, climbing in. Then he turns on his side away from me, pulling the covers back up his body.

I blink at him, still sitting up. "But…isn't there another bedroom?"

"Turned it into the gym slash library. We need exercise and

entertainment. This place is small and as you mentioned, the desert isn't safe." He settles on his back, pulling the blankets back up his body.

"Turned it into a gym..." I repeat, like that's a valid reason for needing to sleep in a room with a complete stranger. "But..."

"Nia," he turns back to me and then pushes up on one elbow. With the moonlight shining through, I can see his rippling muscles, the breadth of his shoulders almost intimidating. And so freakin' hot. Why can't I stop noticing how well put together he is? "I can't have you trying to hurt yourself again."

I stare at him, my mouth hanging open. How did he know? "I wasn't going to hurt myself."

"Really? It looked like you were contemplating—"

"I was contemplating stabbing you," I huff back, not wanting to share the truth. That I know this is likely to end poorly for me and I thought to just get it over with. "If I'd done it, I'd be sleeping alone right now."

He gives me that grin. The one that only lifts one side of his mouth but is sexy as hell and makes my toes curl into the mattress. Like he likes my smart-ass mouth instead of being annoyed by it. "I'm glad to hear you wouldn't hurt yourself, sweetheart. You're far too interesting to leave this world."

I stare at him for several seconds. When has anyone found me interesting? Granted, my world is tiny, and I've never really fit in it. Not since my mom died. I've been completely closed off, but then again, I might have said more to him tonight than I've said to anyone for a very long time.

At first, my extended family was worried about my change in personality. They'd say she's grieving her mother. She's scared.

Then, they just accepted the new me. No one even noticed I didn't have friends. Not real ones.

My friends now are really Jess's friends, and they all have far more in common with her than they do with me. I don't date. I don't go out.

I know it's bad when the kidnapper's compliments are puffing me up, making me feel special. And I'm sharing with him like I haven't talked to anyone in years. What is up with that? Then again, we have been forced into a tiny space together. "I'm interesting?"

I curse myself for asking. Trusting him, opening up to him, makes me so vulnerable, I should have just slit my wrist with that knife. Toni will do way worse to me if he thinks I've betrayed him.

Jake lays back down, lacing his hands behind his head and my mouth goes dry. He's sexy as hell just meeting my gaze in the rearview mirror but like this…

I have this insane urge to climb on top of him. Jesus. I'm losing it.

"Beautiful. Smart. Fantastic singer. A bit of fight. I like that."

My cheeks heat. God, why do compliments from him make me blush? "You like my singing?"

God, I'm pathetic. But even with my plan to earn money with my voice, I've never really shared my singing with anyone.

"Sultry and deep. Your voice is magic." He says matter-of-factly, like he isn't sharing the one compliment I've truly been desperate to hear.

"Can I tell you a secret?"

He turns his head toward me, the intensity of his stare making the hair on the back of my neck stand again. I still don't know if he scares or excites me. Both, I guess. "You can tell me anything."

"I did try to hurt myself once." Why the hell am I telling him this? But that crack I mentioned earlier. The one forming in my hard shell, is growing bigger.

I lick my lips, tasting the words out loud. Is it dangerous to share? My mouth aches at the idea of not sharing the words. And I can't see what it will hurt. It was years ago now…

I see his mouth press into a hard line. "You did?"

I've never told anyone. Maybe I just never had anyone to tell. "After my mom died, the world felt…flat."

I don't tell him that my attempt was after one of Toni's first beatings. I know this is my family's enemy. And as much as I hate my father, I'm not going to actually betray him. Like I mentioned. It's worse than suicide.

"Flat?"

"Like nothing mattered. Especially not me," my voice has dropped to a whisper, and I shiver to remember those feelings. "I was so numb, and I just wanted it to end."

"How long ago was that?"

"Six years," I answer, snuggling deeper into the covers, as I pull them up to my chin.

"So you were fourteen."

"You know my age?" I don't know why I'm surprised as I push up again. He's clearly been studying up on me. Which puts us back in the weird zone.

"It's my business to know about you, Nia."

"Why?"

"Because..." He sits up, crossing his legs on the bed, his elbows coming to his knees, his gaze holding me captive. "We're going to help each other."

"You don't need my help," I shake my head. "Your family is dismantling my father without me."

He shakes his head like he disagrees, but he doesn't say more. "So that was your only attempt in six years?"

I don't want to talk about myself anymore, and I know he's avoiding my question. "How old are you?"

"Thirty-five."

My lips part in surprise. Fifteen years older than me is pretty old. Toni is only forty-two.

I sit up too, mirroring his pose as I lean my elbows on my knees. "You're almost old enough to be my—"

He holds a hand up. "Let's not."

But I cock my head to the side, considering the implications. I've been trying to avoid men in general. Maybe that's why I was never really interested in Gris. It seemed far safer to hide alone than to give myself over to another man and his potential power, even if he could provide protection. What if he abused it the way Toni does?

But now I'm here, having late night conversations with a man who is as sophisticated, successful, and as strong as my greatest tormentor. I haven't been able to trust anyone emotionally. It's such a risk, but what if I could? "Do you think you're strong enough to beat Toni?"

Jake holds my gaze with his. He doesn't move but I feel the change in him. The way he hardens, the way his energy shifts in intensity. "I know I am."

"How do you know?" I nearly whisper this like Toni might hear me. But my senses are suddenly heightened, and some energy is moving through me. This moment feels…significant.

"I was raised old-school," Jake answers. "It makes a man tougher and meaner too. I choose to operate with integrity because control over my emotions, and my actions, make a man strong but that doesn't mean I don't understand your father. That I can't stoop to his level if I choose."

Those words have my heart thudding in my chest. I feel them deeply. Toni never has integrity, and he regularly allows his control to slip, and with it, his empire is slipping away too. While these men…

They grow stronger year by year.

"My father is old-school too. My way or the highway…. I'm not sure it's an asset."

Jake shakes his head. "My nephew Mason has taught me a few new tricks. I know when I need to depend on my family to help me accomplish what I can't alone. I'm never afraid to admit when I need their help or guidance."

They are a strong unit. Jess's words come back to me again about seeking refuge in another family. "What else?"

"And I am crystal clear on how women and children should be loved, cared for, and protected because they are the very heart of an empire."

Something is sticking in my throat. Tears? Emotion? I can't name it and even if I could…I'm afraid of the truth. I lay back down, my thoughts spinning.

Because my kidnapper has made some excellent points and for the first time tonight, I'm wondering if he might be right about this little field trip being to my advantage.

Maybe this situation really could be mutually beneficial.

Or maybe, I am the sacrificial lamb to keep the women they love safe.

CHAPTER EIGHT

Nia

I wake the next morning to find the bed next to me empty.

I push up, rubbing the sleep from eyes as I try to decide what time it is and where my…er…roommate might have gone.

Rising from the bed, I stretch my arms over my head, the clock on the nightstand reading ten in the morning.

My eyes bug out. I never sleep this late.

And granted, I was exhausted yesterday, and up really late, but I was also in a strange place with a strange person. How did I manage to sleep so soundly?

"Good morning, sleepyhead," Jake calls a moment before he sticks his head into the room.

He's still shirtless. In the light of day, I can see every cut angle of him, every pronounced muscle. The smattering of chest hair only making him hotter.

He steps into the room, his hand running down his own body, which is when I catch the flecks of grey in the dark strands of the hair on his chest.

For some reason, this fact instantly makes me wet. What the actual hell?

"Good morning," I say, clearing my throat. I force my eyes away, my gaze going to the window as I stare out into the desert, now shimmering in the sun.

"Hungry?" he asks like he didn't notice me ogling him.

My stomach betrays me with a growl. "Got any coffee?"

"Of course," he answers as he leaves the room again, heading, presumably, back to the kitchen.

I follow, still groggy from the deep sleep. "I never sleep like that," I say with another yawn. If I'm being honest, I've spent years on high alert. How strange that I relaxed with a...stranger.

"I'm glad you slept well."

He's got a blender on the counter, some green concoction all mixed. I wrinkle my nose. "What is that?"

"Smoothie," he answers with a wink. "I worked out this morning and this is how I power back up. Got the recipe from my nephew Leo. His wife is pregnant, and she drinks these by the gallon."

Working out right now sounds wretched. Instead, I take the mug of coffee he offers and take a large gulp.

The caffeine does little to clear my foggy head and the heat of the drink scalds my tongue. Setting it down on the counter, I yawn again. "It's hot. I think I'll take a cold shower and then drink it. That will clear my head as much as anything."

"All right," he answers, pouring himself a large glass of the green liquid.

I wrinkle my nose. "Are you always so health-conscious?"

He chuckles, the sound deep and rich. "Nope. I gave up smoking cigars a month ago, and I drink bourbon the way most men do water."

I stare at him, my gaze drifting down his body. He's joking. Like seriously joking. Except, I caught the faint scent of cigar smoke on his jacket last night.

Heading to the bathroom, I turn on the water and brush my teeth before I shuck off my clothes and step into the cool spray, humming to myself.

Singing has grounded me the last four years. It's the only time I feel alive, whole, worth something. I let my voice grow, swell, my mezzo-soprano filling the bathroom.

It's a funny thing, singing is the one thing I do that is for me.... I wonder if I would actually like making money with my voice? Then it would have to be for someone else. It doesn't matter now. I'm here and not in Canada.

And here is proving to have a few advantages.

This feels wonderful and I close my eyes, just letting the water pour over me for a few minutes as the final notes of my song die and for a moment, I'm just quiet. Nothing but the sound of water.

That's when a strange noise hits my ears. It's like a hissing...

Is it the pipes? We are in the desert. My guess is water pressure isn't the best. But as I turn in the spray, I let out a blood curdling scream.

In the corner of the shower, a snake has curled up, its head lifted, its tongue tasting the air. I scream again, scrambling to get out of the tub but my foot catches the shower curtain and I'm falling, the curtain and the rod come down with me as I land hard on my shoulder.

I let out a moan, pain so sharp it steals my breath, radiating through me.

The door to the bathroom flies open.

This is the second time Jake has barged in and it's completely obvious the lock doesn't work, as Jake stands over me. "Nia! What's wrong?" He growls out above me.

"Snake!" I gasp. "Tub."

"Shit," he rumbles but he doesn't step over me to look in the tub. Instead, he scoops me up in his arms, the curtain and the rod coming with us.

I'm painfully aware that the thin opaque plastic is the only thing separating my naked body from his as he plasters my torso to his bare chest, my arms coming around his neck.

And that's when my shoulder throbs and I give another moan.

"Did it bite you?"

"No," I shake my head, burrowing my face in his neck, the pain threatening to pull me under. "It's my shoulder. I landed on it when I fell."

He stops in the middle our room, looking down at me with a deep, penetrating stare. "How bad?"

I take a cleansing breath, adjusting my arm to check the severity of the injury. "Not too bad," I answer, knowing I'm going to have a nasty bruise, but I don't think I broke anything. The pain is already receding.

He gently sets me down on my bed. "Don't move."

And then he's gone.

I lay there, aware that I'm in a wet shower curtain as he goes back in the bathroom. I hear a loud thump and then he returns. "Snake is dead, though it wasn't poisonous. Just a bullsnake."

He's next to me again, peeling the curtain away from my arm before I can even respond. How is he so damn quick in a crisis?

"What are you doing?" I gasp, though my shoulder throbs again, my wince making my pain obvious.

"Sweetheart," he whispers. "I just want to check you for injuries."

I shake my head. For so many reasons, I don't want him to see my body. First of all, no one ever has. I don't date.

Second, I barely know him and he's my… I can't say *kidnapper* as he strokes his fingers down my uninjured arm. "If it's bad, I need to take you to a doctor."

I look at him then, my brows scrunching as my body relaxes. "But aren't we locked in here…"

"Nia," he whispers, his fingers reaching my wrist and starting back up my arm. "You think I'd keep you here if you were hurt? I told you. I'm a crusty old bastard but not like that. Besides, we're here to help each other."

I melt into the bed, the words disarming even more of my defenses, until I remember the third reason I don't want him to see me. The bruises…

And not the new ones blooming on my shoulder.

But it's too late as he peels back the curtain, revealing my breasts and then my ribs.

But he stops, his eyes narrowing. "What. The. Actual. Fuck?"

I turn my face away, shame making my chest tight. I don't talk, because I'm not sure that *what the fuck* is an actual question. And because I don't even talk about this with Jess. I can't. It's easier to just ignore. Push it down.

"Nia. Did he give you all these bruises? Did Toni do this to you?"

My throat swells and I swallow trying to clear it. I attempt to grab the plastic curtain and pull it back up my body. But he places his hand over mine.

"Tell me, Nia."

I can't. I shouldn't. but I feel the cracks inside growing wider. Dare I bare my hurts to him? "It's only when he gets really drunk. But when Little Anthony got arrested and he found out about the Diamond…"

Jake spits a string of curses that could curl the hair of a sailor. I take it he knows who Little Anthony is. Of course he does. It was his nephew Leo Kincaid who got Anthony arrested.

His hand leaves my arm and then he gently touches one of the large circles that decorates my ribs. "I promise you, he is going to pay for this."

I've forgotten my nudity as I stare at him, my eyes wide. "I don't…" What am I going to say? I don't need him to do that? Don't want him to? Neither are true.

"I'll never let him hurt you again, Nia. I promise."

Stupid tears fill my eyes. I never cry.

"Jake, please don't…" I can't seem to get the words out. I never talk about this. And though I'm sure lots of people in my so-called home know what's going on, no one ever talks about it to me. No on does anything about the abuse. Everyone buries it deep.

"Don't what, sweetheart?"

I can't tell him, don't take this on. It would be a complete lie. Words I least expect come out of my mouth. "Don't tell anyone. I'm so ashamed."

CHAPTER NINE

JAKE

JESUS FUCKING CHRIST.

I'm going to kill him. Slowly. Painfully.

I'm kneeling next to her, one of my hands near the floor, my fist clenching and unclenching as I try to control the rage that is coursing through me.

Tears fall across Nia's cheeks, and I gently brush them away, keeping my touch on her skin light. Easy.

I'm not supposed to be this invested. It's day two for Christ's sake, but she's this mix of strong and vulnerable that is pulling me, literally and figuratively, to my knees.

Toni is taking this beautiful, fragile woman and he's breaking her. I fucking hate it. At the end of this, I'm supposed to let her go. Let her return to her family. Or let her run knowing that the Italians will catch her. She doesn't have the skill to hide from them.

I've got this whole life planned. Start a business. Leave this life. Step away from the darkness that consumed my father, my brother. I can't be her hero.

But the idea of what the Carcettis might do to her after, I can't pretend I don't care.

I've watched abuse. My father, the stupid fuck— I cut the thought short. I will not make this about him.

This is about Toni. But I can still promise Nia this… I'm going to rip Toni Carcetti to shreds.

"Sweetheart," I say in a hoarse whisper, working toward calm. Like I said, my dad was a gangster. By the time I was sixteen, he had me stealing, hustling. By the time I was twenty, I'd shot a man after a bad deal. I know how to be tough when I need to be and I'm not afraid of killing a man.

But Nia's words slay me. I can see the shame in her eyes and feel it deeply. Nia and I are connected, we understand each other in ways I never expected. In some ways, she understands me better than my nephews even, and that scares the shit out of me.

I don't do relationships. Intimacy. I like to believe it's because I'm too hard. But watching her tears, I admit the truth. It's because I'm too weak.

"Promise," she repeats. "That you won't tell."

The whole point of me learning this shit is to tell my family and bring Toni down. "Nia. I can't—"

"Please."

I hear the desperation in her voice, and it twists my gut into a knot. *My loyalty is not to her,* I repeat in my head, but my chin dips to my chest as I stare at the floor.

Gently, she reaches over and touches my hand. "I don't want anyone to know, ever," she says, her words breaking as she speaks them. Or is that the sound of my nerves? Christ. She's cutting me to pieces. "I'm so weak," the words echoing my thoughts, make me flinch, "the only thing I could do was run. And I couldn't even do that…" She turns away and tosses her good arm over her eyes.

A protest rumbles in my throat as my head snaps back up. She survived. She got out. How can she think of herself as helpless?

As awful as I feel for her, I'm also a man, and my objections come to a jarring halt, as I catch sight of her with her arm like that. She's arrayed like Venus.

Her curves are killer and I give my head a shake to clear these thoughts. Instead, I trace another bruise. "You were doing a very admirable job of running away. The fact that Gris Smith is a two-timing bitch is hardly your fault."

"Two-timing bitch?" she whispers but her arm slides from her eyes up over her head so she can turn to look at me again. "He is, isn't he?"

It's a real conundrum because the new position plumps her breasts even more and they are absolutely fantastic.

I don't know why Antonia thinks it's a personal failure that she can't stand up against a hardened criminal who probably outweighs her by a hundred pounds. But I'm big, tough, and I've been part of this world for a long time. I am more than a match for Toni and that fucker is going to pay hard.

"He's too pretty to be trustworthy," I follow up, just trying to ease some of the tension. She can give some of her worries to me. There is a lot I can't promise but I can do this…

I'm going to take all that pain for her. My shoulders are broad enough to handle it and then some.

It works, as she gives me a soft smile in return. "He does look like a human Ken doll."

A chuckle falls from my lips. "Might have made a cute couple considering your resemblance to Barbie."

Her nose wrinkles. "I'm not even close to thin enough."

I fucking love her curves but it's really better if I don't get that specific. Instead, I touch her arm. "Let me have a look at that shoulder."

She shifts and I try very hard to keep my eyes on her face, only sliding my gaze down her neck, and over to her shoulder where new bruises are blooming. "Shit," I mutter. I meant what I said. If she's hurt, we're leaving.

We've got a house not that far from here, fifty miles, and there is a chopper at the ready. I will airlift her out of here if I have to.

Roman is at the house, acting as liaison, while Luke is feet on the ground in Vegas keeping tabs on Toni. Mason and Leo have left with their brides.

We thought about bringing Nia to the family compound that boasts thick walls and a small army of guards. But here, in this tiny house, I've got way more opportunity to really crack her shell, find out what she knows.

I'm regretting the choice now. In this moment, I want her safe even more than I want to know what she knows.

I gently take her forearm. "I'm just going to test your shoulder slowly. You tell me if I need to stop."

She gives a tentative nod and I slowly raise her arm. I've done my fair share of on-the-scene emergency medical care. Another side benefit of being a legit mob man. I know how to tend wounds.

The shoulder seems all right. It moves just as it should, her winces small. Likely, she just bruised it.

I let out a long breath of relief.

"If we left here, where would we go?"

I know what she's asking. She's searching for a way out. Who can blame her? I did steal her. "Family compound," I answer, wanting to make sure she understands she's not getting away, though part of me hates crushing her hopes.

She's been powerless and I just took more of her power. What a fucked-up situation. It's my fault and my doing but I feel myself becoming the one man I never wanted to be. The bad guy.

She winces again and turns away, pulling at the plastic curtain to cover her body.

I place my hand over hers, stilling her movement. Because I can't leave things like this.

She whips her face back, her eyes meeting mine as her blonde hair spills over the side of the mattress and rests on my knee.

"I meant what I said," I start, my teeth gnashing together in my frustration. "When your father is in prison," *or dead,* I add mentally, "all the choices are yours."

She shakes her head. "Maybe."

"You don't think I'll keep my word?"

My fingers are lightly circling her wrist, the softness of her belly under my hand. Fuck, she feels so good. Silky skin. A body lean enough to look amazing without being so hard, that it's not feminine.

She's absolutely perfect.

"Even if you do everything you say," and her voice lets me know it's questionable. "There are seven cousins waiting to be the next Toni. And me? I'll be the woman who betrayed the family. I had one choice. Run."

My mouth opens to tell her I can help her with that after, if it's what she really wants. I don't even know if I'm lying. But she's not done. "And they might have let me go when I hadn't betrayed them. But your announcement of our engagement, it makes me a target."

My head dips and my eyes close because I know she's right. I really have trapped her. I knew this already, but it felt different when I didn't know her. Didn't have the feel of her skin imprinted on my nerve endings. When I thought of her as some mafia princess and not as a beautifully strong woman who has been hurt by Toni too. Maybe hurt by him the most.

Who I am hurting. Fuck. I came here to protect women. Kim. Charlotte. I'm never going to be the man who marries. I'm not the one who builds the empire. But I am the general who defends it. And then I am the man who gets out before it's too late. Before the darkness closes in.

It was just never supposed to be a war against an innocent.

"Let me help you dress." I get up, feeling restless. I'm going to have to work out again. I usually don't even like working out once. I'm just naturally muscular. But with Nia around, I'm crawling out of my skin. I have all this pent-up energy that's just looking for an outlet. Add my absolute need to beat her father into a bloody pulp and I'm ready to do a few rounds in the ring.

"I'm all right," she says, but doesn't move. Letting out the smallest sigh, because touching her isn't going to help, I peel back the rest of the wet shower curtain, pulling the covers up over her body instead. I try not to note the freckle on her hip, the curve of her ass, the dark hair between her legs…

Pushing up, I cross the room and open the closet, a wide array of female clothing hangs on the rod.

"What is that?" she says from her spot on the bed. I make the mistake of looking back at her. She looks just as good from afar, I swear, the roundness of her breasts and hips, her narrow waist on full display underneath the sheet.

I turn back to the closet, trying to cover the fact that my cock just got rock hard. "What is what?"

"All that clothing."

"They're yours," I answer with a small smile.

"They are not mine. I brought two changes of clothes because that was all I could successfully hide in the bushes."

I pull out a dress, spaghetti straps, with a simple floral pattern. Exactly what she likes. Roman helped me with the sizes, not that I'm telling Nia that. But I chose the pattern. It's white with small blue daisies, the exact color I remembered her eyes to be. "I think you're going to need more than two outfits."

She sits up, holding the sheet to her chest, "You really did prepare for this."

My hand clenches on the hanger, we're back to that. I didn't realize just how shitty I was going to feel about what I'd done, taking her like that. What a fucking time to develop a conscience.

"I wanted you to be comfortable." It's lame and I know it.

"I'd like to finish my shower," she says quietly. "Do you think you could clean out the snake?"

"Of course," I answer, carefully laying the dress on the bed. Heading into the bathroom, I remove the evidence, and wash out the shower. I rehang the tension rod then return to the bedroom to get the wet curtain from the floor and rehang it.

She appears with the sheet wrapped around her, her hair gathered over one shoulder. Fuck me, she looks so good, I just want to touch her again, run my hand over her skin.

I want to trace those marks on her body and make them disappear.

I underestimated how tempting being trapped in a small house with a beautiful woman was going to be.

"Shower is ready," I say, my voice rougher than I intended. She steps closer to me, large blue eyes staring up at me with worry shining in them as she nips at her lip.

I want to pull her close so badly my hands itch and I dig my fingertips into my palms. "Will you..." She starts, her gaze darting away. "I'm feeling really anxious..." She shifts, and I can't fight my need to touch her anymore.

I reach a hand up and lightly grasp her shoulder. "What is it you need, sweetheart?"

I feel her tremble. Does she have any idea what she's doing to me? This need to comfort her, protect her, is pulling me as tight as a stringed bow. This is what I wanted, to earn her trust. But somehow, I'm slipping into my web too. I want to protect her as much as I want her to confide in me. "Will you stay right outside the bathroom?"

In answer, my hand still on her shoulder, I reach into the shower and turn on the water. When it's warm enough for her to step in, I finally ease back toward the door, turning my back to her. I don't close the door.

"Want to hear a story about my father?" I ask.

"All right," I hear the sheet drop to the floor and the curtain open as she steps in the spray.

That snake did me a fucking favor, if I'm in the bathroom with her while she showers. I'm still going to have to figure out how the thing managed to get in, though. We can't be showering with snakes.

But this moment, this is more than I could have ever hoped for. And yet, my next words are not just about the game I'm playing. I actually want her to understand me too.

And for her to know, we're way more alike than she ever imagined.

"When I was ten, my pops decided to have a big birthday party for me. All the family and a bunch of my friends. He hired a company to bring in farm animals and everything."

I hear her pause in the shower. She must be wondering where this story is going. Nowhere good is the answer.

"The day was going great until one of the ponies bit me. Drew blood. I started crying because it hurt like hell. What did he do? Punches me in the jaw in front of everyone."

Nia gasps in the shower. I turn back and realize she's got her face peeking out, holding up the curtain over the rest of her like I don't already know what she looks like naked.

Pivoting all the way around, I step closer and touch her face. "The hit was hard enough that he dislocated my jaw. But he wasn't sorry. Told me I needed to man up. Be tough."

"That's awful," she says with a shake of her head.

"I think he thought he was teaching me to be a man. It's how his dad had done it. It was some fucked-up version of love." I'm trying to gain her trust. I really am.

But I also want her to understand. I was her. I bear the same scars. And I know who she is. Which is why I'll be as gentle as I can be.

But also, it's why I can't be her hero. I'm too dark, too close to the edge.

Nia's eyes meet mine. But she doesn't look scared or anxious anymore. This time, her eyes are hard, their blue depths flecked with steel. "Toni's love isn't fucked up, Jake. There is no good intention in his actions. He just doesn't love me. At all."

And then she steps back into the shower and closes the curtain.

CHAPTER TEN

Nia

Over the course of the day, the fear and shame recede. A little…

I think I appreciate that I've met someone who understands what it means to be raised by a psychopath. Then again, Jake might be a psychopath too. He did kidnap me. And maybe I've got Stockholm syndrome because as he sits next to me on the couch reading, I'm glad he's there.

I feel…safe.

Crazy, right? This man is the threat, not the shield. Then again, my father is supposed to be my protector and he's been mostly a cruel jailer. Maybe I don't know the difference.

Maybe shit has been rewired backwards in my head.

Or maybe Jake is different.

I have to will myself to stop thinking about it all. The only thing I should be working out mentally is escape. But I'm sluggish and out of sorts after falling. And Jake learning one of my secrets has made me feel both ashamed and somehow bonded to him, which is dangerous. This is the man I'm supposed to escape from. Not stay with…

Jakes makes dinner and as the sun sets, there is little to do besides go to bed.

I'm tired anyway. Being here, it's like my body has suddenly decided it's time to catch up on all the sleep I never seem to get.

Tomorrow, with some more rest, I'll come up with a plan.

So I go to bed, curling under the covers, my eyes drifting closed.

But I don't fall asleep. I can feel that I'm tired, but some of my old fear is creeping in. What if another snake creeps in the house? The desert is loaded with them.

What if Toni finds me before I can run?

This is my one chance, and I have to make the most of it, because the truth is, if I can escape Jake and this house, he really has helped me just disappear in a way that could keep my father from finding me.

Jake comes in the room and shucks off his shirt, then sits on the bed, removing his shoes.

When he stands, he unbuttons his jeans and pulls them down his powerful thighs, just enough light coming into the room that I can see his body.

God, it's a gorgeous body. The kind that could make a girl forget she ought to be afraid. "Jake?"

He turns around to look at me. "I thought you'd be asleep."

I shrug. "I'm so tired but I can't turn my brain off."

He nods as he climbs into his bed, pulling the covers up to his chest. "What's rattling around your head?" He asks like it's completely normal that I share my inner thoughts with him.

"How did you recover? From your father?"

He's silent for a few minutes. "I'm still not sure I have."

I nip at my lip. "What makes you say that?"

"I did just steal you in the night. I'm not exactly winning any good-guy awards."

For some reason that makes me smile. "Do you really think you're helping me?"

"Yes," he says without a moment of hesitation. "Toni would have found you within two days if you'd gotten on that plane."

That makes me sit up. I want to deny it but I'm sure he's right.

Look how easy it was for Jake to take me. I've got to do better the next time. "So I'm doomed?" But Jake doesn't need to know I'm already planning the next time...

"You can let me take care of you," he says, looking back at the ceiling. "I'll do a much better job than Toni."

"What does that even mean?" Take care of me? I lay back down, frowning at the ceiling. I don't know that I'll ever trust a man after what I've been through. I can't even give affection to my sister. Then again, Jess hasn't been through what I've been through. She doesn't know what I know...

"It means," he whispers softly into the night, "that you could become a Kincaid."

I gasp, sitting up as the spaghetti strap of my tank top falls down off my arm. "You're not serious."

"I am," he says and then he props up on one elbow, his lean body on full display in a way that makes my mouth go dry. He's so tempting...

I shake my head slowly. This can't be real. He abducted me to propose? Even stranger, I think I might actually be considering his offer.

I lay back down, flopping onto my pillow. "This is crazy." My uninjured arm goes over my head, and I stare at the ceiling. I don't want to marry into another Vegas family. I want to go far, far away. Find my own place in this world and never trust a man again.

The room quiets and I shift, trying to stop my swirling thoughts.

"Nia," Jake finally says. "I can hear the gears in your head grinding."

I push back up, wanting to ask him what a marriage to him might involve. Wanting... "I..."

"Come here," he says and then he lifts the covers back from his bare torso, a clear invitation.

My mouth goes dry. There is a part of me that's so tempted. "Jake," I stutter out. "I..."

"We're just going to sleep. I worked out three times today and I'm exhausted, but I doubt I'm going to bed until you do."

I only hesitate for one more second before I'm pushing off my twin and stand in the small space between the two beds. I'm in a short tank and a pair of bikini briefs but it doesn't seem weird at all, as I slide into the little bed. I know you're not supposed to snuggle the man you're trying to escape. But I was up against him today, and he feels good. I can't deny that.

And as much as I know Jake should be one stepping-stone on the path to finding my way, I need to get my feet back under me, and drawing from his strength sounds like a really great idea.

He extends an arm and wraps it around my torso as I settle into the space next to him. He pulls me close against him, my skin slides against his.

I almost moan at how good his rougher skin and hard muscles feel. No one told me about this. I hear the other girls talk about sex but never about intimacy or how just touching a man like this is so…erotic.

About how even laying against a man with his arm around you can make a girl's brain kind of fritz.

My hand comes to Jake's chest, my fingers flexing on one of his pectorals before it slides over his muscle as I test its shape.

"I did say you were just here to sleep," he murmurs, sounding completely relaxed.

I lift my head. "That marriage you offered up, are there any other perks besides safety?" I should not be asking this question, but he feels so good.

His head jerks to face mine, his eyes dark and intense in a way that steals my breath. He half turns toward me, his other hand cupping my ass cheek and pulling my pelvis tighter against his hip. "You want a few perks, sweetheart?"

My mouth goes completely dry. I should have known that Jake is not the kind of man you tease. He's an alpha. Used to getting his way and shaping what doesn't conform to his wishes into exactly what he desires.

I can fool myself that I'm trying to use him but, in this moment, I know, I'm putty in his hands.

He slides his palm down the back of my leg, until he hooks my knee and then pulls my leg over his. It pushes my aching sex deeper against his hip and I give the smallest gasp.

But he only looks away, closing his eyes. "Go to sleep, sweetheart. It's too soon for anything more than that."

See. There he goes, thinking that he's going to dictate exactly when and how things happen between us. Granted, he's commanded my every move, but that doesn't mean...

I feel my eyes closing.

Because as good as he feels, I'm exhausted too. And what I need more than to prove him wrong by humping him, is to get some sleep, and make my brain work out a plan for getting out of here and starting on my own life.

Allowing myself to trust him too much would ruin me forever—well, any parts that aren't damaged beyond repair.

Next to him, however, I fall asleep within seconds.

And I don't wake up until Jake moves me. "What time is it?" I slur into his chest, that I'm still using as my pillow.

"Seven," he answers, tightening his arm about me as he lifts me and then slides me under his body.

My eyes jerk open, a little gasp falling from my lips, but he keeps moving, as he stands up and stretches.

I let my gaze slide up the power of his thighs, his narrow hips and lean waist, over the rippling muscles of his chest and broad shoulders.

I lick my lips as he leans down and kisses my forehead. "I'm going to work out. Feel free to go back to sleep.

"All right," I stretch in the bed, knowing that I'm not going back to sleep. "Can you leave me a cup of coffee?"

"You got it, sweetheart."

I rise from the bed, stretching too, my arms over my head, my hip out to one side.

He stops, going still, as his gaze slides down my body.

I lift up on my tiptoes, extending even further into the stretch as I partially turn away, showing him my profile, my ass sticking out.

I don't know why I'm teasing him like this...

Except I remember how he tried to dictate all the terms last night and I feel the need to try and gain a little power here. It's a dangerous game. He's got way more experience than me, but I've never even been tempted to tease a man this way and part of me can't resist.

I know it's a dangerous game. I'm even sure I'll lose but…I love the heat of his gaze as he takes a step closer to me.

I'm covered in his scent, the feel of him still fresh in my memory as I pivot again, my back facing him as my arms stretch out from my sides.

"Nia," he says, his voice so full of gravel that the ache between my legs pulses. Maybe I need to work out today too. I'm clearly amped up.

I look over my shoulder, giving him a sweet smile. Is this bothering him?

His face is set in hard lines, the cords of his neck standing out as the heat of his gaze nearly sears me.

And suddenly it occurs to me how I might distract Jake…find my method of escape. It's a shit plan because every time I think I have the smallest bit of control, he takes it right back, but it's all I've got.

And besides…the man is too delicious to ignore. I've never had a chance like this and who knows if I will again.

And yes, I'm totally justifying.

With a deep breath, I drop my arms just enough to run my palms over my hips.

He takes a step closer, a rumble erupting from his throat. "You know that I'm the predator here," he growls, one of his hands fitting into the curve of my waist.

He's right. I'm completely inexperienced, a captor, and apparently, a slave to my impulses.

But I just need to feel his skin on mine again.

CHAPTER ELEVEN

Nia

Before I can even answer, he's got his other hand on my waist, and I'm bent over the bed, the length of his erection fitting against my ass.

The hard edges of it feel so good, I moan even as my face presses into the covers.

I've still got my underwear on, he's in his boxers, but the thin cloth does little to dim the pulsing ache that he's causing as he presses deeper into my flesh.

His hands slide up my ribs, pulling the straps of my tank down my arms with a quick motion that frees my breasts in a second.

Before I can even gasp in a breath, he's got them both in his hands, tweaking my nipples as his palms hold the weight of them.

I let out another moan of pleasure as he gives each of them a good hard squeeze as he pushes our hips together over and over. The friction is sending tendrils of excitement pulsing through me.

Pleasure is building, the ache so much more intense than anything I've ever experienced. He's still holding my breasts in his hands, using them to pull me closer as he pumps against me.

I fist my hands in the sheets just riding the pleasure for all it's worth. My body is spiraling higher as he pumps harder, and I know I'm going to break soon.

No one explained this one to me either.

He's not even inside me. How does it feel this good?

I'm whimpering, pushing up on my tiptoes to feel even more of him, my thighs beginning to tremble as I get ready to cum.

But that's the moment he lets go of my chest, stepping back.

I cry out a protest as I lift my head. I need him back against me, I'm so close to the best orgasm of my entire life...

I look back over my shoulder just in time to see him yank down his boxers and my eyes go wide.

I had no idea that this man's erection would be so...amazing. And a little scary too because I have heard Jess's friends talk about the size of cocks a lot, so I know for a fact that Jake is big.

My mouth opens and closes as Jake's hands come to my hips and he yanks down my panties until they're around my knees.

And then he's got his hands on my hips again, his erection pressing right against my opening.

That's when the fear zings down my spine.

"Jake," my voice comes out as a croak, tight with worry.

He stills, his hands still holding my hips, but the pressure instantly softens. "Yeah, sweetheart?"

The way he says it, it makes me relax again. It's been fast and just a touch rough in the hottest way possible, but he's still Jake. He's in control and he doesn't sound angry, more concerned.

"I just...I wanted to tell you..." I draw in a breath, even as one of his hands comes up to my hair, brushing it to the side and over my shoulder. It's so tender that I reach for his hand, holding it in mine. "I've never done this before."

His fingers jerk from mine, his eyes going wide as his mouth parts in surprise. "You're a virgin?"

Regret lances through me. I don't want him to stop. I'd like nothing more than to get rid of my virginity. It feels like some hurdle I should clear before I try and make it on my own.

And weirdly, I trust Jake to be considerate about the whole thing. Which is so telling. With my body, I trust this man. "It doesn't change anything," I cry. Starting to push up from the bed. "I don't want you to stop."

"I'm not taking your virginity doggy-style with a hot, fast fuck," he spits but one of his hands comes between my shoulder blades, pushing me back down.

I start to resist, not letting him press me into the bed. Did he just say he wasn't going to….

But, before the words come out of my mouth, his other hand settles between my legs as he rubs his fingers through my lips.

Now he doesn't need to push me back down, I go willingly, my ass in the air. I'm dripping wet as I push into his hand.

He rubs up and down me again, inserting one finger inside me. "Christ, Nia, you're so fucking tight."

"Is that bad?"

"Oh sweetheart," he murmurs, pumping his digit into me. "It's so fucking good, but it's going to take a bit of adjusting before I go shoving my cock inside you. I'm not beginner-sized."

I'd laugh if what he was doing to me didn't feel so good.

He slides his finger out, putting his thumb in, the rest of his hand settling in the crack of my ass in way that only makes me hotter before he bends down and takes a long lick right over my clit.

My entire body jerks with how good it feels, the orgasm already building.

"Oh my God," I whimper as he starts to swirl his tongue over my clit.

I don't care that I'm probably way in over my head. Don't care that he has all the power as I grind against his face. "You're so delicious," he murmurs into my pussy before he sucks hard.

I let out a whimpering cry that sounds like a half sob, as he pumps in and out of me. And when his teeth graze my clit, I lose it, cumming so hard my vision blurs.

But Jake isn't done.

Surging up, he's flipping me over onto my back with a single arm. I don't even have time to react, the move showcasing every rippling muscle before he's on top of me, sucking one of my breasts into his mouth.

"Oh," I moan out, burying my hands into his hair as I press him closer.

But he resists the pressure, moving over as he takes the other nipple into his mouth. He tugs the tank further down my torso. "You're going to ruin the set," I laugh as the tank rips in his hand.

But he doesn't laugh back. Instead, he relaxes back, tracing one of the bruises on my ribs. "I'm not scaring you, am I, sweetheart?"

I blink back at him. Scare me? I've never been less scared in my life. He's strong and his movements are all power, but there is no anger in them. They are controlled in a way that leaves me free to enjoy without any fear. "Not at all."

"I know what your father has done," he starts, skimming his hand over another bruise.

"Toni's not my father," I shake my head, not wanting Toni to be part of this at all. "But you can be my daddy."

His hand jerks away, his mouth thinning into a hard line. "Nia."

I know I'm working out some kind of issues. I don't think about it too hard as he straightens up, standing next to the bed.

Because his cock is still rock hard and now it's leaking the smallest bit of fluid. "When it drips like that, is that like me? Is it because you're excited?"

"Nia," his voice rings with a warning, but I'm not scared of him. Not now.

I slide up and then pitch forward, flicking my tongue over the liquid collecting it from the tip onto my tongue, before I pull it back into my mouth. I want to know how he tastes.

My eyes close as his salty essence hits the roof of my mouth. I like it.

I hear him hiss out a breath. "You taste good, Daddy."

"Fuck. Me. Stop calling me..." But I lean forward, running my tongue over the small slit in the head of his cock before I place a soft kiss on the tip. "Yeah, sweetheart," he groans, his head tipping back, his earlier remonstration forgotten.

In answer, I do exactly what he did to me, I lick and then I suck, grazing him with my teeth.

"Where did you learn to do that?" he hisses.

"You taught me," I answer, licking him again before I slide my mouth over the head and take more of him into my mouth.

"I taught you?"

I slide off, looking up at him. "Just now. I'm doing what you did to me. Do you like it?"

He stares down at me, his eyes dark and dangerous, but they don't scare me now. In fact, they make me even hotter as I suck more of him, sliding my lips as far down his cock as I can go.

He's rumbling incoherent words, his hands sliding into my hair as he pulls me further down on his cock.

I take him in, loving the feel of his fingers in my hair and on my neck. I love how I've stolen his words, that he wants me as much as I want him.

I swallow as much of him as I can, choking a little but I am so past caring. This is more than I ever imagined it would be.

His thighs begin to tremble, and I know that means he's close. But I don't want this to end.

I've never felt more in control of anything than I do in this moment, and I ease back, looking up at him.

His hands tighten in my hair. "Sweetheart, I need—"

"What do you need, Daddy?"

CHAPTER TWELVE

JAKE

IF THE CALLS me Daddy one more time, I think I might just cum all over her face.

The nickname shouldn't be that hot, but it is.

She's kneeling in front of me, her big blue eyes staring up at me, her mouth puffy and red.

My cock throbs again, more cum leaking from the tip. She flicks out her tongue, licking the drop of liquid away like she actually likes the taste.

Fuck. Me.

"I need you to put my cock back in your mouth." I don't even tell her not to call me Daddy. I can't. I like it too much.

It's dangerous territory. I've promised to care for her. I'm lying. Maybe.

But as she tips forward, sinking her mouth back on my rock-hard erection, I realize she may very well be rewriting my lies into truth.

I bury my hand into the thick strands of her blonde hair as my addled brain tries to unravel why Nia is different.

Why is she making feelings I thought dead surge inside me? I don't have any answers as my cock hits the back of her throat, her cheeks puffing out as her eyes get wider.

Jesus Christ, it's so hot I can barely stand it and I'm leaking more precum right down her throat.

How can a girl with this little experience be this hot?

As if to double down, she places her small, pale hands on my hips and holds me in her mouth, keeping me from pulling back out.

It's the final straw and I fucking break hard, my cum shooting into her mouth, down her throat as I spasm, my jerking motions creating just enough friction that I cum even harder.

I don't even know what I'm saying but I'm spitting words as I tighten my grip in her hair.

This was not the plan.

The plan was a slow, steady seduction that was sweet and loving. I want Nia to fall in love with me, spill all her secrets.

I've been taking great pains to be gentle…careful. I already knew she didn't have much experience.

I didn't expect her to be a virgin. Everyone knows her sister Jess gets around despite the strict rules the girls live under.

I didn't expect to feel anything at all for Nia. She was supposed to be the enemy. Instead…

I digress. I expected Nia to be inexperienced enough that I needed to be a gentleman. Be slow and sweet.

Instead, I'm cumming down her throat as I spit and roar, my balls so fucking empty that I just want to collapse back in the bed.

I pull out of her mouth, my chest heaving as I stare down at her.

Her underwear is still dangling around one ankle. Her torn tank around her waist.

Her chest is rosy, her cheeks flushed, her eyes sparkling with a bit of water from the effort of keeping my monster cock in her mouth.

I can't help it.

I bend down and kiss her hard, my tongue ravaging her swollen lips before it tangles with hers.

This is not the first kiss I had in mind at all. But I can't stop myself as she tips back, laying on the bed.

I follow, covering her body with mine, my cock already getting stiff.

How can that even be possible? I just had the most amazing orgasm and yet…I want more.

I twine my fingers in hers, lifting her arms over her head as I settle my hips between her legs.

My cock is pressing into her still-dripping folds and I grit my teeth. I can't take her virginity now.

I need to slow this train. But I don't want to think about my fucking goals or my stupid plans. I just want her.

I want to fill this woman with my cum. As if she hears my thoughts, she wraps her legs around my hips, the softness of her thighs so warm and sweet I groan into her mouth.

"Are you going to make me yours, Daddy?"

There isn't a doubt in my mind that I am going to make her mine. But I don't have to do it all in one day.

Do I?

Part of me is already aching to be inside her. But I need to focus on the long game and not throw it away for a bit of pleasure.

No matter how much I want it.

Nia is a little vixen and that could be to my advantage if I'm careful.

My forehead falls to hers. I don't want to be careful. I want to say fuck it to everything, bury myself inside her, and worry about the rest of the world later. "I am, my little sweetheart. But not just yet."

She mewls out a protest, her hips rolling against mine. "What if I asked with a pretty please?"

She is pushing every one of my buttons and for a moment I have to wonder who is playing who. It's sobering enough that I push up, looking down at her rosy face. Her eyes are a bit unfocused, a flush still on her skin.

I place my hand over her heart, feeling its wild beats. "How many boyfriends have you had, sweetheart?"

She blinks up at me, slow, like she doesn't understand before her tongue darts out to lick her lips. "None."

She's got to be lying, right? My cock doesn't think so. It gets even harder, pressing into her slick folds.

Because part of me knows she isn't. I've watched her. No dates until Gris. No public outings.

And there is so much she's completely naïve about. I know she's telling the truth.

She rolls her hips again and the head of my cock starts to sink inside her heat.

But it's not long before it stops, her tightness keeping me from going further.

That and the tensing of all her muscles.

I immediately retreat, pulling back out. Nia is going to need some stretching and I shouldn't rush this anyhow.

She needs time, we need trust, and I need…information. "Baby girl," I start before I softly kiss her lips. "We don't need to do it all in one morning."

She nods, her eyes wide, her features tight. "I didn't expect it to hurt that much."

I'm easing up, pulling her with me. My cock gives a needy throb like he didn't just unload.

"Why haven't you dated?" I ask as I stand, pulling her into my arms and carrying her toward the bathroom.

Since we're already naked, we might as well shower. And this way, I can check it for any critters.

She shakes her head. "I think you know enough already to know that I've been afraid."

I look back at the bruises peppering her body. I know about that. And I hate myself all over again. She's struggled to trust in the past and by some miracle, she's starting to put some faith in me.

Part of me wants to cherish that, celebrate it. But another thought niggles in the back of my brain, something she said that I ought to remember despite the haze of lust, but I can't call it back.

I get in the bathroom and turn on the shower, Nia craning her neck to check the tile floor. I chuckle. "I promise I won't let you shower with snakes again."

She gives me a shy smile. "Going to keep me safe, Da—"

"Nia," I rumble out because my cock is fucking jumping again.

And then it hits me. What she said... Toni wasn't her father. Did she mean that in a "he's dead to me" kind of way? Or is he really not the man who sired her?

Which makes my arms tighten.

Because my brother had an affair with her mother. It's what got him killed and it's why I am going to make certain Toni is punished.

"What?" she asks innocently with a sweet little smile. She knows the nickname is getting under my skin.

I take a deep breath. My brother slept with Maria Carcetti a decade ago. A full decade after Nia was born. I let the air out of my lungs in a long rush.

So, not my niece. Thank fucking God.

But I do remember my brother telling me that sex with Maria was like nothing he'd ever known.

Is it hereditary?

It doesn't matter. I push those thoughts aside for the more important ones. The ones I'm here to find out.

Because as much as I'm starting to feel like Nia is the person I need to protect, I'm here to help my family.

"Bad little girls get spankings," I rumble. What the hell is she doing to me? I've been keeping it light, gentle, easy.

Easing her into this. But we just plunged into the deep end. Only Nia doesn't look scared. "Is that as hot as it sounds?"

My jaw clenches as I step into the shower and immediately set her down in the hot spray, turning her so that her back is to my front as I nudge her feet further apart.

Nia has this flat toned belly that's gorgeous, but she's got a real flare to her hips and a plump round ass that nestles my cock as I pull her tight to me.

I'm not spanking her today. Hell. This is a woman who's really been hurt. But a little dirty talk...

"The way I spank, you're going to love it." I slide my hand down her belly and through her hair, only stopping when I'm cupping her pussy.

And then I give her clit a light smack, the water cushioning the slap so that she sucks in a breath and then moans. "Oh yeah," she hisses as I do it again. "Spank me more."

My answer is to plunge two fingers into her tight pussy.

Her knees buckle and I wrap my other arm around her to hold her up. "Tell me the truth, Nia," I'm rumbling into her ear. "Do you want to be mine?"

"Yes," she moans. "Oh yes."

I'm pumping my fingers in and out of her, the heel of my hand grinding into her clit.

"And you're going to be a good girl for me so that I make you cum over and over?"

"Yes."

I want that so fucking bad too, but I know I'm playing her right now. I'm close to learning something crucial and I can't forget why I'm here. Where I'm going…

She's getting close, I feel her trembling, and I slow my hand. She lets out a cry of protest even as I rumble in her ear. "Promise me, sweetheart. Promise me we're going to be good to each other."

"Promise," she gasps and then I add a third finger, stretching her out and getting her ready for when we kick this party up a notch.

She starts to cum the moment I hit that spot inside her pussy, her legs giving out as I hold her up and pump in and out of her while she gasps out another orgasm.

My cock is starting to weep too, the needy bastard so ready to be buried inside her.

She's limp against the shower wall, her body so placid, I kiss the back of her neck.

She stirs a bit, picking her head up. "That was… Wow."

I smile into her skin. "I agree."

I reach for the soap, beginning to scrub her down and ignoring my own raging hard-on. Because the way I extract the next piece of information from Nia has just occurred to me and it's perfect.

I know that her mother had an affair with my brother a decade ago. But by pressing that issue, I might be able to extract another truth.

Which means my little man is going to have to wait.

CHAPTER THIRTEEN

NIA

JAKE RUNS his hands over every square inch of my skin, not missing a single crack or crevice.

I'd be embarrassed but I'm too satisfied.

Dimly, I wonder what just happened. It's like every reservation, every inhibition fell away the moment his thumb skimmed over my nipple.

I can admit that I've been dying to have a man touch me. I just didn't want any of the other complications.

After everything with Toni, I've been afraid to date, frightened of giving a man power. But with Jake…

It all just fell away.

The heat between us burned the fear, turning it to ash and dust that blew away as the fire of passion blazed.

I know what happens with fire like that. It consumes everything. I'm not a complete idiot. But I also don't know how to make it stop.

Because after two orgasms, my body is humming again at the feel of his hands.

Growing up, I heard the rumors about my mother. They called her a siren. A woman of intense passion and skill. And those are the nice words.

I was too young to know if it was true. She was just my mother.

I know that Toni was completely infatuated with his wife. Jewelry, flowers, lavish vacations. Until it all came crashing down.

I can only guess that he was devastated by her betrayals. Part of me even understands. But that doesn't excuse what he did to her, or to me.

Jake's chest presses to my back, his hands are on my belly. "You drifted away there for a minute."

I shake my head. "Sorry. Just thinking."

"About?"

I nip at my lip. It's one thing to decide to let Jake give me mind-blowing orgasms. I've never trusted a man before and I'm just going to go with the fact that I've let my guard down when it comes to being physical.

But trusting my family's enemy with family secrets...I don't know that I'll ever be ready to go there. I can't forget how we got here.

"Nothing," I answer.

"Nothing."

"The usual..." I look over my shoulder at him as he holds my hips in his hands. This is the part where I have to be very careful.

"Usual?"

"Wondering whether or not I should have let my kidnapper touch me like that."

His brows lift as he squeezes my hips tighter. "Too late for regret."

His hands slide up to my waist and they nearly span the entire way round. I've always had a small waist, a real hourglass figure.

Does Jake like that? I banish the thought. This is about making him relax, creating enough room for me to escape. Maybe.

I flex my hips. Pushing back into his pelvis. "You're right. Way too late."

"You could drive a man mad, you know that?" He pulls my ass tighter into the cradle of his hips.

"Really, Daddy?" God, I love calling him that. It makes my pussy ache every time.

He rumbles in my ear. "We need to talk about that."

"Don't tell me you don't like it?" I whisper out, my voice breathy, which is no act. How can I want him again?

"It has its charm and we both know there is some truth there. That I am not your kidnapper, I'm your protector."

The words cause a tingle that touches every nerve ending in my body. My protector. That would require a different kind of trust that I don't know I could give. Still, I'm tempted. I'm ready to admit that.

"Jake."

He kisses that spot just under my ear. "Earlier, you said that Toni wasn't your father."

I stiffen. Shit. Did I share that?

I was so hot in the moment. I knew I shouldn't play this game. He's got so much more experience than me and I am clearly losing if I'm sharing details like that.

"I just meant…"

"Considering your mother and my brother had an affair—"

I gasp, turning toward him. "What?"

His mouth thins. "They had an affair. It's what got him killed."

My eyes blink several times. Toni killed his brother? Is that why I'm here? Jake said it was because Toni was attacking their women, but these things always have a beginning.

I've paid attention long enough to know that. Nearly every aggressive act I've witnessed is the tenth, eleventh, twelfth in a long line of acts that have created deep wounds.

I swallow down a lump. "Your brother was killed?"

"Gunned down in the street. His son Leo was with him. It was Leo who held him as he bled out."

I don't really know Leonard Kincaid, I've only seen him from afar a few times. "I'm sorry for Leo," I say, but emotion is clogging my throat. Because I know all about watching someone you love die.

But that memory is the reminder of where placing your faith in the wrong man can take a woman.

So I push my sympathy back down, drawing several deep breaths. It's like I pick up the pieces of a suit of armor and slowly, I put each piece back on, hardening myself, putting my feelings away.

He studies my face, his head cocking to the side. "No one should have to watch that kind of shit."

"No, they shouldn't." I push away from the wall I've been leaning against, shuffling around him to get out of the shower. I don't want to be this close to him anymore. My insides are turning dead again, my emotions closing like turning off a faucet.

But his hand shoots out, grabbing my waist. I shrink away, a gut reaction. I've gone into full duck-and-cover mode.

"Hey," he whispers, his hand softening but not letting go. "What's going on?"

"I want to get out of the shower," I huff out, my voice tight. "I need some space…I…"

"I'm not going to hurt you." His fingers gently brush my skin. "I promise. Protect. Help. Satisfy. Apply those words to me."

It's very tempting, but so dangerous.

"Enemy," I return. "Make sure to add that one."

His jaw goes granite-hard. "I am your father's enemy, but I am not yours."

"You took me, Jake. Like the pawn that I am." And then I twist away. He lets me go this time and I step out of the shower, wrapping myself in one of the towels.

Tears prick at my eyes as I wrap my arms tighter about myself. I'm not even sure what just happened. Why I suddenly feel so vulnerable. Unsafe.

"You're not a pawn, sweetheart. I took you off the board. You get to go be whatever you want. Stay here, be my wife. Go and start a whole new life."

My shoulders deflate and one of the tears I'd felt pricking at the back of my eyes slips down my cheek. He sees it and wipes the little bit of water away with the pad of his thumb.

If there is one thing I've felt with Jake, it's been cared for. I'm not sure what changed in the shower, but the gentle touch reminds me of why I grew comfortable in the first place. But it also helps me focus on the moment. I lost that feeling. "What's with all the questions about my mother? About Toni?"

His head cocks to one side. "Your mother. My brother. While I like you calling me Daddy, I'd be less fond of uncle."

My eyes go wide, and I gasp in a breath. Because. Yeah. That's a really valid reason to be asking about my mother.

"Your brother is not my father," I whisper and then I flick my blonde hair over my shoulder. "My mother's a brunette. All of the Kincaids have dark brown hair."

"So does Toni." He reaches for the wet strands, letting them slip through his fingers. I swallow down a lump because he's hit the very heart of it.

It seems dangerous to tell my father's enemy that I'm not actually the daughter of the man he wants to hurt.

But honestly, I'm bad enough at this game that I don't know how it might come back at me. Will it make me less valuable? Would he let me go? Or just throw me away? "Yep. Toni has dark hair too."

"My brother wasn't your mother's first affair."

It's the tone of his voice. It's changed. Even with his hands on me, it's grown harder, developed an edge. I don't like it. "If you want a detailed account of her sexual conquests, I was a child. I wouldn't know."

"I'm not looking for a list, Nia. I just..." But I turn again, starting for the bedroom. I can feel more tears welling in my eyes.

"I look like her, you know." I toss over my shoulder. He knows that Toni beats me up. I'll let him decide if that means Toni loves me more or less. But I'm done talking about this. I'm done talking to him.

And that thing we did this morning. Pretty sure we're done with that too.

Which is a shame. As a girl who has always been caged, when Jake was touching me, I've never felt freer.

CHAPTER FOURTEEN

Jake

I know I fucked it up.

I did not learn what I was after in terms of information, but that isn't even what's bothering me.

Today, I watched a beautiful woman start to come alive under my fingertips, and then I scared her right back into her shell.

Fuck.

I hate that I scared her. Hate that I hurt her.

I don't know what's happening to me. I've spent a decade dreaming of revenge on Toni Carcetti.

I've plotted, and planned, and punched my way into this position. And Antonia Carcetti, my sweet, innocent temptress, is dismantling my dreams and reshaping my intentions one blue-eyed glance at a time.

How do I explain to her that lately, I could feel myself slipping into the abyss that I'm sure consumed my brother. I'd stopped caring about life. I'd wondered what it might be like to let the darkness take me.

That's why I'm getting out.

Nia's right about what her family will do to her if they find her. But if I claim her, I'm never leaving this life. I'd have to stay to keep her safe.

But the thing is...when I'm with her, the world is far brighter.

I want to trace her curves far more than I want to hurt anyone, including her father.

I enter the bedroom to find her under the covers of her bed, the blankets pulled up over her head.

Fuck.

Not even bothering to dress, I pivot and head out to the kitchen, making her a cup of coffee that I carry back into the room.

Beneath the blankets, she's softly crying.

"Sweetheart," I croon, sitting on the edge of the bed. "I've brought you that coffee."

"All right," she says, not coming out.

"Come have a sip. It will make you feel better." I reach down to touch her but stop, not sure if I'll make things better or worse.

"I don't think coffee solves this problem," she answers, but she stirs under the covers.

"It'll help." I rest my elbows on my knees, using my index finger to rub that spot between my eyebrows.

I know what I want from Nia. What's become less clear is the consequences of taking information from her. I'm trying to find my path forward. Which way keeps me from following in my brother's footsteps? Helps my nephews? Betraying Nia or protecting her?

I'm starting to feel as stripped bare as she is. "New story," I murmur my eyes still closed.

I hear the covers rustle.

"Three years before my brother died, my father just disappeared. At that point, he was in his sixties and not really part of the business anymore. He was never found. One day there, the next day...poof."

She gasps and I open my eyes to find her just peeking out from the covers, her red-rimmed blue eyes staring at mine. I reach over and stroke my thumb over her cheek.

"What happened to him?"

"Don't know," I shrug. "We have no idea if it was an old vendetta, a random act, an accident, or a decision to just leave."

"How did you feel?"

I don't talk about my feelings. Ever. But this is about trust and giving to get, and I know I have to tell her the truth. The moment I started pushing my agenda, she shut down. "Our relationship was complicated, but he was my father. I hate not knowing..."

"I can imagine."

"And that's the thing about this morally bereft life. Eventually, it swallows us all, I think." I don't tell her I'm trying to get out. But before I do leave Vegas and all its trappings behind, I'll do the job I know my nephews don't have the darkness to complete. My heart speeds up in my chest and I rub at my breastbone.

"You think it will swallow Toni too?"

The fact that she's talking about Toni is perfect. And I get far more information out of her for sharing about myself, but I feel the bonds between us tightening. "Sooner rather than later."

I need to remember why I'm fighting, and she needs to know it too. If Nia is going to help me, she's going to volunteer what she knows, I'm not going to extract it.

"He always seemed invincible to me."

"No man is invincible. Three years after my father disappeared, my brother was gunned down."

She nips at her lip, her hand sliding up my biceps in a clear sign of comfort. I meet her eyes then, wanting her to understand. "And Mason, he came to us with a plan to make us legitimate. No more guns, no more violence. It wasn't that simple, but we've mostly lived it. And I honestly thought it might save us. Me and my nephews."

She stares at me.

"And then," I whisper, leaning closer. "Vendetti bombed Mason's building while Charlotte was inside."

Nia gasps, and I slide my fingers into her damp hair at the base of her neck.

"And little Anthony put a gun to Kim's head."

Her eyes go wide. "And that's when the rules changed. Because

Kim and Charlotte, they are our family now. Our women. And we are their soldiers."

She nods like she understands. I lean close enough that my forehead comes to hers. She doesn't pull away. If anything she leans into me, our breath mingling. "And when a woman joins our family, she gets the full weight of our protection."

I kiss her lips and she doesn't skirt away. Nia needs to feel protected. Safe. Who can blame her? But that's how I win her. I don't even question why I want to win. Is it my war or her betterment?

Instead, I kiss her again. "I offered to marry you, sweetheart. If you accept, you get the entire Kincaid family as your soldiers. Understand?"

She nods, this tiny movement.

I draw in a deep breath. I'm so close…so close to attaining what I've wanted all this time. But I can't even think about it now. The fresh scent of soap and the soft slide of Nia's skin fill my senses. Am I hurting her? Making her real promises? It's all twisted together.

"And I promise you. We are not criminals. Not like your father. We run a legitimate real estate empire. Yes, we work with families like yours. Mostly, Mason loans them money to keep them in check. The one exception to our legitimate life is…"

But it's Nia who answers. "When the people you love are threatened."

I run my fingers through her hair. "That's right."

"Why do you want to know if Toni is my father?"

My teeth grit together. She isn't ready for the truth. Her being a witness against her father puts a price on her head that I'm not sure I can protect her from. She's already in so deep…

My offer of protection is mostly fake. It makes my fingers tighten in her hair, my stomach twist into dissatisfied knots. I want to make it real. I do. But first, I need the information I came for and then I can figure out if I can keep her safe.

"How hard is he going to fight for you?" I ask, my fist clenching into my side as I wait for the information I was always here to collect.

She shrugs. "Hard. He'll come for me because I belong to him, because he has plans for me."

I sit up, staring down at her. What kind of plans? I clamp my jaw together to keep from asking.

Because I'm back to caring more about Nia than about my family's plot to remove Toni forever. And also, I had no idea that Nia had a purpose in the family. I took her because she has information. How bad is this? How much have I hurt her. And my family? Is this going to blow back on them? A brick settles in my stomach.

"But if you're asking if he cares for me, I doubt it. I'm just a tool." She fingers a lock of her own hair, which is drying, the blond becoming increasingly apparent.

"He's not your father." I don't ask. She doesn't have to say anything.

She shakes her head. "No. It was a tennis coach, I think. I've seen one picture. Blond hair, blue eyes." She shrugs.

I'm trying to decide how I determine the plan that Toni has for Nia. But before I ask, she takes another sip of her coffee.

"I know you offered to marry me, Jake, for my protection. But it isn't good enough, no matter how much money your family has. Not unless you'd be willing to forgive the debts my father owes, and I know you won't."

I stare at her, trying to make sense of those words. How would Nia bring in enough money to get her father out of debt?

A niggle of understanding snakes down my spine and a rage begins to build in my chest. The piece of shit wouldn't...

"If you told me you could make me disappear, like witness protection, that would be different. But I doubt you can."

"Why would you think I couldn't?"

"I should have said, *I doubt you will*. Because all I can I figure is that I'm here to act as bait."

I keep my face expressionless, but inwardly, I grimace. It's not far from the truth.

She looks away, setting her cup on the nightstand between the beds. "Toni is no man to underestimate. He'll kill me and he'll kill you too if he finds us."

She wraps her arms around herself as I slip off the bed, resting on my haunches so that our faces are level. Does she understand that if I do what she asks, I'd be losing the witness I need?

I'd be giving up my future, the one where I get out of this life and maybe the future of my nephews. They need me to do what they can't. Shamelessly use an innocent woman who is the one person who is still alive who can prove Toni Carcetti is a murderer.

I'm facing a decision that means her or the safety of my family. "So if I let you go, for example, Toni does what with you?"

"He marries me to some mob boss in Italy."

Fuck. My hand is on her hip before I can stop it, like I'm going to physically hold her away from Toni.

"And if you protect me, then I'm assuming your plan is ruined."

I don't answer. She hasn't asked me what my plan is, not that I'd tell her. But Nia has always been intelligent, and she's realized, without knowing my plan, that we are at an impasse.

I have to choose her, my family, or come up with a new plan. I stare into those big blue eyes as she nips at the shell-pink full lips.

"So, Daddy? What's it going to be?"

CHAPTER FIFTEEN

Nia

It's not like I didn't know he was pumping me for information. But, as much as I've given up in terms of knowledge, I've gotten some things out of him too.

His gaze holds mine, his gray eyes wary and alert. Cold. And I already know, he's not choosing me.

I get it. We've known each other a few days. But that means I can't let what we did this morning lull me into this false sense that he's my hero.

He isn't.

I've got to save myself here. Does he even want me at all? The idea that what we did this morning is all part of his plan makes my chest ache.

I don't know why I let it hurt. I'm just a tool to Toni. Something to be used and discarded. Why would it be any different here?

But the idea that I'm just something Jake is using makes me stiff with anger.

Tossing the covers back, I'm still in my towel as I scoot past him, grab my coffee, and head to the bathroom.

Might as well blow out my hair.

Because I'm in a war and if I'm going to fight him, I'm going to look good doing it. But that makes me pause.

Maybe I'll work out first...

I pull open a drawer and pull out a sports bra and shorts, setting them on his bed. Then...I drop the towel.

I hear him growl behind me, but I don't look back. Instead, I grab a pair of bikini briefs from another drawer and bend over to slide them on.

He growls again. Louder.

The sound pulses through me and I swear, my clit gives an aching throb.

I doubt I'll win at a game of seduction, but it's the only play I've got until I can think of another.

And like I said, I've learned some useful information. This is a chess match of revenge and Toni is the target.

Does he suspect that Toni is behind his father's disappearance? Lifting my arms over my head, I pull on the bra and then the shorts.

Grabbing socks from the drawer and sneakers from the closet, I leave the room without a word and cross the hall into the makeshift gym.

I've been in here a few times to grab books, but this time, I head to the treadmill in the corner and sit down to pull on my socks and tie my shoes.

Jake appears as I stand, workout shorts slung low on his hips.

He comes over and stands next to me and the machine, pushing the power button and then two more to make the treadmill start under my feet.

I nearly slip and fall but his hand shoots out to grasp my hip as my feet catch up to the belt. The heat of him nearly sears me as my cheeks fill with color. I grip the handles and start moving, intentionally staring forward, not meeting his gaze.

"You didn't wait for my answer," he quietly says as I start walking.

"I didn't need to. I already know," I answer pushing the up arrow to make the machine go faster.

His arms cross over his chest, making his biceps bunch up in the sexiest way. "Nia."

"Jake."

"No Daddy?"

I shake my head. "That's the name for a man who is actually caring for me, isn't it?" Foolishly, a few more tears prick my eyes. Why does my stupid heart want me to be wrong? I know I need to be on my own, not trust a man. I've known for a very long time.

"I told you that I would take care of you."

"You did. But I'm not sure why I should listen." I feel him draw up. His shoulders straighten.

"I'm salty. I drink too much, and until recently, I smoked too much. I never tell people I care about them, and my favorite form of communication is sarcasm."

I step off the belt of the treadmill, resting my feet on the side rails to turn and look at him. "Okay."

"I've hurt people, and I've done a few shady deals. Including taking you the other night."

My heart is thudding in my chest as I finally look at him, his gaze holding me captive.

"But one thing I am not is a liar. So when I tell you I'm going to protect you no matter what, I will."

And then he turns and walks away, leaving me in the gym. The belt runs as my feet rest on the sides, and I stare after him.

I know I shouldn't let him sway me. He's been in command this whole time, and this is likely just his next play to keep me where he wants me.

But I'd be lying if I didn't say that part of me wants to chase after him, tuck myself against him, and let him be the wall that breaks the danger that surrounds me. Or maybe he just breaks me.

I shake my head, and step back on the belt.

I need time to think and time to plan and I can't let my insecurities, my past pain, push me into a place of weakness.

So instead of chasing him, I turn up the treadmill.

I have no idea how long I run but when I get off my legs are jelly.

Leaving the gym, I find a plate in the kitchen with a large southwest salad already made.

I stare at the food, wondering if I should eat it. I'm so hungry, and I'm not worried that he's tampered with it. But him making me every meal is one more way in which I am under his protection, his care.

Then again, who wants to waste food? Opening the fridge, I pull out a large bottle of water and take a few swigs.

Sitting down, I slowly begin to eat. I know what I need to do. I need to slow down the explosion of chemistry that happened this morning.

As much as I think I've gained, he definitely came out the winner. He's been in control the entire time, and he still is.

With that in mind, I finish my salad then enter the bathroom, checking for snakes myself before I take a shower, rewashing everything, even my hair.

Wrapped in a towel, I blow it out, putting on more makeup than I usually would.

It's not Jess-level, but it is more than just lip gloss and mascara. I wish my sister was here.

I'd like to tell her that I love her. I haven't said the words to her in so long.

With a sigh, I make my way into our room, picking out a dress for the day. I hear the treadmill start.

Was Jake waiting for me to do his workout? Are we avoiding each other? Works for me.

We stay in our separate corners all day and then the next.

We barely talk. We don't even eat together.

And yet, I've never been more aware of a person in my life. I've got to come up with a plan and get out of here.

Because, by the third day, the tension is so thick, I think I might break…

CHAPTER SIXTEEN

JAKE

THERE IS no amount of working out that could take the edge off my tension. And I don't even like working out.

In fact, until this little adventure, I hardly ever touched the inside of the gym.

Now, I'm in here constantly and I still want to rip the world apart.

Or maybe I just want to rip off Nia's panties and plunge tongue-first between her thighs. She was so fucking delicious. Sweet with the perfect amount of musk. I've been dreaming about her taste.

She's not talking to me, but she is walking around the house with the smallest amount of clothing possible, hair and makeup making her look even more like a Hollywood starlet on vacation.

And the little dresses she's been wearing…

They hug her curves, highlighting her flat stomach and her lush ass.

I keep replaying our morning together, over and over in my mind. I know that Nia isn't experienced, but that woman turned vixen in my hands, and I want her again, the way I want my next breath.

I'm increasingly thinking of her and not of what I'm here to do or what might be happening back home.

I'm sure the guys can sense it. Maybe it's my silence, but I'm not surprised when I get a text from Mason saying that he'd like to talk this evening.

The meeting is scheduled for two in the morning, Mason understanding that I'm in a very small space with Nia and that late at night is the only time I have an opportunity for privacy.

I respond with only a thumbs up as I hear Nia leave the bathroom. I'd been cutting up fruit while she's been working out. When she entered the bathroom, I'd stopped entirely, just listening to the shower, remembering how I had her pushed up against the wall, her ass against my cock.

When the door clicks open, I finally come to my senses and start chopping again.

None of my nephews would believe it, but I actually like cooking. The act is somehow soothing, and I like it even better when I'm feeding Nia.

I can't explain why giving her nice food makes me happy.

Though the idea of being in the kitchen with her makes me a little crazy. It's a small space and I'm ready to break.

I know she'll want breakfast and coffee, but everything in me clenches as she enters the kitchen with her hair and makeup done but still wrapped only in a towel.

It's barely long enough to cover the generous curve of her ass, as she walks in and takes the cup I've poured her.

She drinks one sip, pauses, and then bends over to get the sugar out of the cabinet on the island.

I lean back, getting the barest peek between her legs as she bends before she is straightening back up.

If she isn't careful…

I had my cock cradled against those sweet cheeks once and I would give anything to bend her over this counter right now and—

"Thanks for the fruit," she says and grabs a piece from the bowl I've left and pops it between those plush lips.

The tiniest bit of watermelon juice coats her lips and all I can think about is licking it off. I press against the counter, discreetly adjusting my now-stiff cock as I don't respond.

I've spent the last few days considering how I protect Nia and still exact my revenge on Toni.

She's right about her family. If her marriage was supposed to save the Italians, they'll see this as a betrayal. Especially since I took great pains to make it look as though Nia and I left Vegas together and ran off to get married.

I wonder if anyone even suspects that I forced her against her will. She was in the act of running away, packed a bag, stored it in the bushes.

I didn't know she was doing that. But that doesn't matter now. Her family is never going to forgive her.

She comes back out of the bedroom in a pair of short little shorts and a tank. I lean against the counter and watch her as she slips onto a stool and lifts another piece of fruit, pineapple, and pops it into her mouth.

Even her chewing is sexy, and I cross my arms, committed to just watching her eat. It's sexy as fuck and I'm a starving man.

"I feel like I need a little sun," she says after a few more pieces. "You?"

My brows lift. That's it? Suddenly we're talking about taking a stroll together? I've spent the last two days, when I'm not admiring every part of her, racking my brain on how I help my family and get her out of this mess that I've landed her in.

"Outside?"

She pauses, her mouth open, a piece of kiwi in front of her lips. "That is where the sun shines."

"What about the sun porch?"

She wrinkles her nose. "Not the same."

My brows cock. I know she's up to something. I can't have her getting hurt now. And I can't give her the chance to try and run. Tonight I'm going to pitch a plan to Mason. We get Nia's taped confession for the police, and then Nia and I disappear.

I'm still not the forever guy, despite my proposal. That was as much about convincing her to trust me as anything else, but that doesn't mean I can't spend a year protecting her, helping her establish a new identity, while my family finishes neutralizing the Italians and bringing them to heel.

But to explain that I'll take her away but not marry her means I might have to come clean about my original intentions.

Nia is not a woman who trusts easily, and I'm going to kill any trust I have left, which is not much. I know that.

"You want to go out now? It's got to be one hundred and ten degrees out there."

She nips at her lip. "It's a dry heat."

I shake my head with a chuckle. That's Vegas's favorite line next to, *What happens in Vegas...*

"A little sun?" I ask, watching her closely.

I see the light that sparkles in her eyes. She is definitely up to something.

"A little sun."

"All right then," I push off the counter, moving around the island to take her hand.

Pulling her toward the door, I stop to swipe my finger over the invisible pad.

The lock clicks and I feel her fingers tightening around mine.

Was she hoping to learn how the door worked? She'd have to cut off my finger to be able to use it on her own. I've wired this place myself and I'm the only one who can operate the house.

Good thing the knives are now firmly tucked away.

We step into the heat, my skin instantly growing sticky. "So much for dry," I mutter.

A small smile tugs at her lips. "It feels wonderful."

"Like to be hot?"

"The sun warms you up when no one else will," she answers and lifts her face to the sky.

Maybe this was her plan. Because my chest tugs at the admission of loneliness in her voice. And I find myself wanting to promise to keep her warm for a long, long time. Fuck me.

There are a few old chairs, left over from construction, leaning on the side of the house and I grab them, unfolding each one and setting it in the dirt. She slips into one and I take the other.

The sun actually does feel nice. I won't make it more than thirty minutes but it's nice to get a little vitamin D.

"So, what do you do when you're not stealing young women?"

I shake my head, really enjoying the return of a bit of banter. "Excuse me, Miss Sassy, but you are the one and only young woman I ever intend to steal."

She laughs. "I see. Want to know something about me?"

"You know I do."

"I actually do a fair bit of this at home. Sitting outside despite the heat. Jess thinks I'm crazy."

"So why do you go out then?"

"Makes me feel less trapped."

My gut clenches. "You're his prisoner too." And that's what I hate. I'm him. My father. Her father. The realization hits me like a punch to the gut and my stomach clenches.

I've trapped a beautiful woman by my side, one that I know is going to get hurt.

I can't stand it. I can't be him. With startling clarity, I know I can't be another Toni. I can't be cruel like my father.

"Have been for a long time." Then she turns to me, her cheeks the most beautiful shade of pink as her skin heats. "I've thought about it."

I stay silent having no idea what she might say next.

"And I'd rather that you killed me than send me back to Toni."

It's like she dropped a cement block on my chest, and I stare at her wondering if I'll be the one to vomit this time. Mason's wife Charlotte made a similar request of Mason.

There is grit and then there is inner strength and an understanding of the dark side of life. I've got both.

But by slow degrees I've learned, so does Nia. We are so alike in so many ways. Forged from the same fire. She understands me in ways even my family does not. "I am not killing you, Nia."

"Please," she whispers, leaning closer. "You were right about a few things. I've had time to think here in ways that I never got to at home. I'd rather be dead than return to that life."

I turn to stare out at the desert. "You're not going back, and I am not hurting you ever. I already made you promises, and I meant them."

She reaches for my hand then, her small fingers slipping into mine, her pale skin in such contrast to mine. "I'm scared, Jake."

"Don't be, sweetheart," I hear myself whisper back. "I told you, I'm a crusty old gangster and I am plenty man enough to make Toni pay."

"I'm sure you will. But that doesn't mean I won't pay too."

My eyes close. "You and I have both been forged by fire. Haven't we? We understand the prices that must be paid for every choice we make or…someone makes for us."

"You're not wrong," she whispers, her voice raw. "But you know that phrase, out of the frying pan and into the fire?"

"Yeah."

"I can't seem to tell where the pan ends and the fire begins." She stares off into the distance, her features pulled tight with tension.

I tighten my hold on her fingers, knowing it's time to make the picture clearer. "Want to hear another story?"

"Yes."

This time, I don't need her to share anything in return. I just want her to understand. "You know that time I told you my pops broke my jaw?"

"Yes," she answers.

"My mom had to take me to the emergency room where they put the jaw back in place. Lied and said that I'd fallen off the pony that had bitten me and that's how I dislocated it."

Her other hand comes to mine.

"Then, when we got home…my pops had this collection of baseball cards he loved. Some of them worth a lot of money. She took them out in the backyard and lit them on fire."

I hear Nia gasp, but I don't look at her. "He beat her up worse than me, but she did it knowing how much he'd hurt her after. It wasn't a pretty home. But my mom, she had my back."

"Where is she now?"

"Nursing home. Dementia," I answer as I look back at her blue eyes. "I don't want to do what they did. That fucked-up marriage. But my mom, she is the one person I could always trust to stand up for me, Nia. Not until Mason did I have another person I could really count on. I won't abandon you, Nia. I promise you that. And if I break that promise, you can kill me, sweetheart."

She stares at me as I turn my face up to the sun. "We can stay out as long as you want. Just tell me when you're ready to go in."

"Just a few more minutes," she answers. Despite our sweaty palms, her hand stays in mine.

I mean the promise. I've changed and I can't change back. I don't want to.

I'll die before I let Toni or anyone else hurt her.

I close my eyes, feeling the heat of the sun, the prickle of sweat.

The air is growing thicker. When I open my eyes, I see them. Giant plumes of clouds that are sure to mean rain.

Storms in the desert can be dangerous. With a grimace, I tug on her hand. "We should head inside."

"Why?"

"Storm," I point at the clouds. "And it's going to be bad."

CHAPTER SEVENTEEN

Jake

Did I say bad? I meant fucking awful.

Torrents of rain begin to fall within fifteen minutes of us retreating into the safety of the house.

The thing about the desert is that it goes so long without water, the dirt gets so hard-packed, it can't soak in any of the water.

The house is fine.

It was made for these kinds of rains, a waterproof membrane making it tight and a pump pushing the water away from the foundation and into a storage system for the house.

I watch from the windows, knowing that the cisterns we've put in place will be full after a storm like this, giving Nia and I all the water we'll need for weeks.

We'll also get some rare desert flowers. Maybe Nia and I can even take a short walk tomorrow. I know she'd like some more time outside and maybe it will be a chance for me to tell her some of the truth.

I can't keep it from her much longer. She's too beautifully imperfect and though I know I'm never going to be the long-term guy, there is this part of me that's starting to want... But, I'm no one's Prince Charming.

I think I could be her dark knight. The one that slays her dragons and hides her in my castle until the danger has passed.

I can save her.

My thoughts swirl as I watch the rain pelt the windows, the storm mirroring my own tumultuous thoughts.

And that's when the power goes out.

Nia is sitting behind me, draped over a chair, legs dangling over one side in the most tempting way possible when it goes, the pop and then the silence making her give a little cry. "What was that?"

I step closer to the window, squinting out into the rain. And that's when I see it.

The solar array's connection to the junction box has pulled free. We won't have power back until it's fixed.

I hesitate for a moment.

Without the burning sun, we can go without the air conditioning.

But the pump system…

Letting out a curse, I stomp toward the door.

"You're not going out there?" Nia cries, standing too. "It's pouring and the wind is just awful."

"I'll be fine," I answer, turning back to look at her. Her long legs are on full display, her body a temptation that never fails to make me pause. But her eyes, filled with worry, are what really capture me now.

In two quick strides, I cross back to her, and pull her against my body, bending down to steal a kiss.

I shouldn't.

We haven't touched in two days, but I can't help it now. Her worry for me breaks some final straw. I can't stay away.

Her lips are soft, and so achingly sweet that I groan into her mouth. The kiss lingers, are bodies pressed tightly together as her hands reach up and wrap around my neck. "Don't go out there."

I kiss her again, pressing my forehead to hers. "You need light to read."

"I could sing instead."

"I definitely want to hear you sing," I answer with a smile. "But the house could flood."

She gives a tentative nod as I slowly back away. "Have a towel ready, would you?"

Nia nods, and disappears down the hall, as I turn toward the door. The piece is basically a plug. I knew I should have hardwired it in.

Opening the door, I stomp through the ground water, crossing the twenty-five feet to the edge of the panels where a small shed holds all the batteries that store the energy.

Yanking the cord, I bend down, fitting it back through the opening in the shed and inserting it into the box.

I hear the batteries fire back up, the air conditioning unit a moment later. Standing, I give the cord a triumphant grin a moment before I turn back toward the house.

But another giant gust of wind blows just as I turn.

I hear the sound of ripping metal a moment before something whacks me in the back of the head.

Pain explodes in my skull as I fall to my hands and knees.

But the only thought I have echoes in my head.

Nia.

CHAPTER EIGHTEEN

NIA

THE POWER COMES BACK ON, just as I pull a few towels from the closet.

I look up, giving a bit of a cheer.

It's silly, but I have to be honest, I'm in a bit of a silly mood. After two days of tremendous tension, our talk outside, and then that kiss, has soothed the rough edges. I still don't know where Jake and I stand, or what he wants to know from me.

But in that moment when I was afraid, he kissed me, held me in his arms.

Deep inside, I just think it means something.

I'm a fool. I know it. But my body has been aching for his touch and my thoughts have played on infinite loops of questions until I can't think any more.

I just want to feel.

I head back out into the kitchen and living room, catching sight of Jake by the corner of the house.

The wind hits his back, the rain soaking his shirt, but he has a grin on his face that matches my own.

Is he glad the tension has broken between us? Or just happy the power is back on?

I watch as he turns, but I instantly gasp as a strip of metal rips from the solar panels, catches the wind, and heads right for Jake.

A scream rips from my throat, but he can't hear me through the rain and wind.

It hits him on the back of the head with a force that sends him to his knees.

Dropping the towels, I race for the door, yanking the handle. I don't even question why it opens as I run for Jake, my bare feet splashing through the water.

"Jake!" I scream into the wind. "Jake!"

"I'm all right," he calls back, trying to stand, before he sinks back down. "Or I will be in a minute."

Reaching him, I bend down too and wrap my arms about him, giving him a tug.

He lets me pull him up, but I tighten my grip when he sways. "I've got you," I murmur. "I'll help you inside."

He wraps his arm about me, stumbling with me back into the house. The moment we're in the entry, I close the door, pushing out the rain and the wind. My arms are still around Jake when I realize...

I'd just had my chance.

I was outside. He was on the ground.

I could have run.

He leans more heavily into me, his forehead dropping to mine. "Jesus. I didn't see that piece coming at all."

Next to me, an alarm sounds a song, its beeping supposed to sound melodious. But it only rings harsh in my ear. A robotic voice calls from the wall. "Alarm system rebooting."

I blink, looking at the small box next to the door. "Alarm system engaged."

"Nia."

I draw in a harsh breath. I was outside. He was on the ground.

I know I'm repeating myself but I just... How could I save him instead of myself?

He takes a step back, staring down at me. "What's wrong?"

I shake my head. I just made a choice. Was it incredibly stupid? I don't even know. "I just…" I look at the door.

He must understand because he takes another step from my side and grabs the handle, his thumb passing over the pad. Then, he swings it open.

I'm instantly hit with rain and wind, the water pricking at my skin.

"If you want to run, Nia, run."

My gaze jerks to his. "What?"

"I won't stop you."

I shake my head. "You won't?"

"But I will follow."

My shoulders curl at the words, my head dropping down. "Because I'm your prisoner?"

"No."

The single word rings through me, snapping my chin back up. "What is that supposed to mean?"

He steps close again, the door still open but his body blocks the wind, the rain. And then he leans down, lightly grasping my chin as he kisses my lips again. "Because. You're mine to protect."

I stare up at him.

I made a choice. Without thinking, I chose him. Would he choose me too? Is he choosing me now?

I've never wanted to trust a man, I've always been afraid.

What if I can't choose a man who is good for me? What if I'm too broken?

But with Jake…for the first time in my life, I want to try.

He's probably the man I should trust least of all, which is why alarm bells are ringing in my head. Am I picking the one man destined to be as bad for me as Toni?

Maybe.

But I shake my head, knowing that I'm going to stay. "Close the door."

CHAPTER NINETEEN

Jake

My head aches all day, ibuprofen only dulling the pain. After Nia checks my injury, we go back to avoiding each other. Something has shifted and I know we're both grappling with what that means.

I've made promises to my family, to my dead brother, and I'm going to see them through. Besides, my brother Frank was my protector as a child and it's my turn to give back to him.

Frank should have never gotten married. My nephews are a huge part of my life, but their parents, my brother, that was some crazy shit. If I ever thought I'd make a relationship work, Frank taught me we're too fucked up for happily ever after.

But when I look at Nia, I want to be a different man…

At nine, she just goes to bed.

I lay there listening to her breathing slowly, it grows deep and even.

I wish her head was on my chest.

I pull out my phone, setting an alarm for vibrate and then lay it on my chest, but I never fall asleep. My head still aches and I feel torn in ways I never expected.

I wait for what feels like an eternity and then get up, pulling my laptop out from under my mattress where it's been tucked.

Mason was alerted that the systems in the house went down, and I know he's going to have even more questions.

I don't bother with a shirt as I make my way into the gym and softly close the door.

Firing up the computer, I open my email where I find a link to start our chat. I'm fifteen minutes early but I open it anyway and then start browsing Vegas news.

A rash of crime has hit the city and if I were to guess, the Carcettis are behind it.

Mason appears five minutes before our official start. "Jake."

"Mason," I answer my nephew, sitting back in the chair. "What's the word?"

Mason grimaces. "It's ugly."

Shit. My hunch was right. "Tell me."

"I could start with how I'm currently living with Leo and his very loud sex life," Mason wrinkles his nose as Leo appears on the screen.

"I fucking heard that," Leo spits. "And I don't know where you get off telling me that my sex life is loud. I heard the spanking you gave Char—"

"I meant, what's the word in Vegas," I interrupt, sure that Mason and Leo could explode on this call if I let them. They are brothers and they love each other fiercely, but they mix like oil and water.

Mason sighs. "We closed the Diamond."

"How pissed is Toni?"

Leo scrubs his face, his ever-present stubble scratching into the microphone. "He bombed one of our buildings. Again. Small pyrotechnics, but we had to shut the casino floor of the Starlet down."

"What else?"

Luke appears on the screen, the chat shuffling as he settles into his chair looking more tired than I've ever seen him. His dark hair is a mess and there are dark circles under his eyes. Luke usually has a devil-may-care attitude, but he's the one man who stayed in Vegas while the rest of us have scattered and I can tell he's taking the heat. "Are we discussing Toni's crime spree?"

Roman jumps on the call too, the compound lanai in the background. I can say one thing, Nia would like that space. "What are we discussing?"

"We've only gotten as far as the bombing," Leo interjects with a frown.

"The good news..." Luke smirks. "I had cameras installed everywhere with automatic backup of the footage every thirty seconds. Not only did we get several of his henchmen on camera before he shot them out, but we got Toni with them two minutes before the bomb went off. He's being investigated by the FBI as we speak."

My brows lift. I may not have to get Nia to confess to anything. Toni is going to put himself in prison. I know the rest of her family poses a danger to her as well, but with Toni behind bars, my attention and my loyalties will no longer be divided. I won't have to choose to make Nia a witness and my family will be safe from Toni.

Granted, the rest of the Italians might want my head and Nia',s but I made that problem when I put that announcement in the paper.

"Jake?" Roman asks.

I snap my attention back to the call. "Anything else?"

"We're considering moving you and Nia to the compound."

"Why?" I like being here with her. And while the compound has way more security, it might also be a place someone thinks to look. Here, we are completely off the grid, tucked far away.

"Toni's turning over every stone to find her," Mason answers. "And I mean every stone."

Luke winces. "We didn't expect him to be this adamant. He's offered the other family's major real estate to get her back, he's had men in all the competitors' establishments causing trouble, and he called Mason making all sorts of threats..."

"Like that would work," Mason snorts. "But he's going to keep trying until he lands in prison or..."

"Someone gets really hurt." Inwardly, I grimace.

"Is it because of what she knows?" Leo asks like I'll have the answer.

And I do. "Oh, she holds all kinds of secrets."

"She sharing with you?"

I nod, and then poke my fingers into my eyes. It feels wrong to share our private conversations with them. Which is so fucked up because that was the whole point of bringing her here. So I don't talk about her mother or the way Toni hurts her. Instead, I share what impacts them the most. "Toni's made a deal with a foreign family. They're going to pay top dollar for her to marry some high-up."

"Fuck," Mason grunts. He's the smartest of the bunch so I know it's even worse than I thought by his reaction. "It's probably not just a payout but a guarantee of business and labor. It's Toni's move forward to get out from under our debt and keep his family in the game."

I can hear his worry. "Does that mean she's in real danger?"

"It means…" Mason shakes his head. "We meant to take a pawn when we took Nia. But instead, we captured the queen." He runs a hand through his hair. "And whoever holds her at the end, wins."

Roman taps his fingers on the table in front of him. "We should move her here as soon as possible."

I shake my head. "Is there any indication Toni is closing in? Because if not, I'm making really good progress here."

"What else have you learned?" Mason asks, cocking his head to the side.

I have learned a lot but not just about her. I'm coming into focus too, not that I'm telling them that. In fact, I don't want to tell them any of it.

"Your father wasn't Maria Carcetti's first affair," I murmur pushing my fingers deeper into my eyes. I feel like I'm betraying her, and I take a breath, trying to decide how much more to share when I hear a strange thumping in the house.

I go silent, lifting my head and sharpening my focus.

"What's wrong?" Roman asks quietly. As the man closest to me geographically, it's his job to ask the question.

But I don't answer, as I hear the noise again.

Is Nia in trouble? My chest swells, my hands curling as, without warning, I slam down the laptop, stuffing it between some towels in the workout room.

The muffled noise sounds again, even as my phone starts to blow up with text.

What the fuck happened?

Where did you go?

Is everything all right?

Pocketing the phone, I move into the hall, cocking my head to listen. I hear it again. It's clearly coming from the bedroom. Nia is in trouble. I rush forward, knowing that I'll do anything to keep her safe.

I grab the door handle, but that's when I hear it…a soft moan.

My teeth grind together. Adrenaline pumps through me as I toss open the door, thoughts of Toni and the danger to Nia driving me forward.

But the moment I'm in the room, I stop.

Nia lies in the bed alone, her eyes closed. Her head thrashes to one side, a low moan falling from her lips. "Jake," she softly whispers as her leg kicks out, crashing into the footboard of the bed. "Daddy."

And that's when I look down and see her hand between her legs.

Is my little girl masturbating while she dreams about me?

A jolt of sexual energy like I've never known pulses through me. She's been tempting me for days but I'm not the only one who is tempted. Even in her fucking sleep, I'm who she wants.

Well, little girl, ask and you shall receive….

CHAPTER TWENTY

NIA

I KNOW I'M DREAMING.

I've had my fair share of sex dreams, and a girl can always tell. They are filled with wanting but light on satisfaction.

This one is no exception.

I can practically feel Jake's hands on me but he's not touching me where I need it most and my body is aching to explode in orgasm.

"Nia," his deep growl reverberates through me, so real, I jolt in surprise, waking from the dream.

My eyes fly open, and Jake stands over me.

His chest is bare, but he has athletic pants on. "Jake?"

"What's wrong, sweetheart? You were crying in your sleep."

I blink at him, my mouth opening and closing. "Was I?" I finally push out between panting breaths. The ache is still there, the pulsing need. I look down to see my hand is buried between my legs, nothing but a sheet covering the evidence that I was dreaming about the dirty things I want him to do to me. "Bad dream. That's all."

We're in some sort of battle. He's the last man I should want touching me. But I've applied myself to teasing him the past few days.

And while he still seems perfectly in control. I'm dying to have his hands all over me.

And he knows...

"Bad dream or good dream?" he asks and then he reaches for the sheet, peeling it back from my body. I freeze, blood flooding my cheeks as the sheet skims over my belly and then lower, revealing my hand buried inside my panties.

He lets out a rumbling growl that makes me pulse with some deep need and my fingers flex to push deeper into my folds.

And then I arch my back because it feels so good and I am so close.

"Please, Jake," I whisper, not even sure what I'm begging him for.

"You want to cum, baby girl?" He brushes my panties to the side, his middle finger sliding into my sopping-wet pussy.

"Oh God, yes," I gasp out my body already vibrating with an impending orgasm as I brush my own fingers over my clit again.

"Who's your daddy, baby?" And then he slides out, pushing a second finger and hitting that spot that has my whole vagina contracting.

"You are," I say without hesitation, spreading my legs wider. I want my clothes off, I want his mouth on my nipple, I want...

I gasp as the first orgasm slams through me. It was so fast, I'm barely even prepared. But lucky for me, Jake's just getting warmed up. Pulling his fingers out, he yanks my panties down my legs and then lifts me up, pulling the tank over my head.

It's a tiny bit of fabric, as I'd made a show of climbing into bed in my scantiest pieces. The tank top rips as he pulls it over my head, landing in a jagged pile on the floor, as his mouth clamps down one of my nipples. I cry out at the electric tingle that pulses through me as his fingers slide back through my folds, teasing me again.

But he doesn't tease for long...

His mouth is nipping and sucking down my torso kissing a trail that sets me on fire.

When he kisses the place where my leg meets more torso I shiver with a bit of a tickle, but he only growls into my skin. "You smell so delicious."

And then he takes one of my knees, parting my legs as he settles his shoulders between them.

Taking one long lick, he sucks my clit between his teeth. I scream, another orgasm slamming into me.

Christ, the man barely needs to do anything and I explode.

He jolts up and shucks off his pants, his erection jutting out from his body. I don't feel the least bit afraid as I stare at his thick cock.

If anything, I squirm in anticipation. I want to know how it feels…

I sit up, reaching for his hip and pulling him close, my mouth opening as I let his cock sink between my lips.

He moans out his satisfaction, his head falling back.

I don't know what happens to me when we touch, but it's like I become this completely other person. Bold. Alive. I want him to touch me in every way imaginable.

I can't get enough and I sink deeper until his cock hits the back of my throat. Even then, I'm holding his hips in my hands, keeping him close.

"Sweetheart," he grates, his voice ragged.

I wait another second before I push back, my mouth leaving his cock with a little pop. It's messy and so hot. I look at him, knowing my eyes are watery and there might be a bit of drool on my lips. "I want you to take it."

His dark gaze holds mine, his jaw going granite. "Your virginity."

It's not a question. He isn't asking. He bends down, snaking an arm under my behind and then he lifts me so that my bare chest is pressed to his. And then he kisses me, long and slow, a completely different tempo and pace from what we've been doing.

I melt into that kiss.

Because as hot as everything we just did was, when he kisses me like this, it's my heart that he touches.

Crap. That isn't supposed to happen.

This is why young little virgins can't play with grown men. I'm so far over my head here. "Please," I beg, wanting so much more of him.

He kisses me again. "I know, baby girl. I know..." I've already wrapped my arms around his neck, and he lays down on the bed so that I'm on top of him.

I can feel his cock pressing into my heat and I wiggle the slightest bit, letting a bit more of him sink in.

It already burns, and my eyes widen in surprise.

Everything we've done has felt good. But I know this is going to hurt.

His hands come to my hips, but he doesn't pull me down onto him, instead he holds me still. "But tonight, I don't want there to be any pain," he whispers against my lips. "Tonight, I just want to make you feel good."

My eyes close as he kisses down my neck.

"Only good." As much as I want all of this man, it's a tempting offer. "How would we do that?"

He's kissing back down to my breasts, sucking on one first and then the other nipple. "Fuck, you're so beautiful. Do you have any idea how perfect you are?"

I shake my head, too busy enjoying how the scruff on his chin feels, the way his teeth scrape as he sucks.

It's just the right amount of pain to make the pleasure more intense and I'm arching into him.

His hands skim down my back and over my ass, one of them settling in the crack. For a moment, I stiffen, but he only runs his finger along the seam, circling my little brown hole.

My eyes widen at how good it feels, how it amps every bit of pleasure, making it more intense.

"That one is mine too," his low gravelly voice reverberates through me. "Every part of you is going to be mine."

"Yes," is all I can say as he takes my hips again and starts to lift me away from his body.

I cry out a protest but he only grins.

"I could use a bit of satisfaction too, love." He's still pushing me up and settling me next to him. "So why don't you spin around so that we can help each other."

"Spin around?" I have no idea what he means. But his grin only turns more wicked.

"Come sit on my face," he says, his voice so rough, I give another pulse of pleasure at the sound alone.

"How is that going to help you?" But I'm already pushing up to my knees, climbing on top of him, settling my thighs around his head as I brace my hand against the wall. Curious? Yes. Excited? Absolutely. Do I trust him with my pleasure? Completely.

He gives me a long lick, swirling his tongue right where I need it most. I'm so ready to ride him that I grab one of my own nipples, giving it a pinch.

But he grabs my wrist, stopping me.

He lays his head deeper into the pillow, giving himself enough room to speak without being muffled. "I'm going to need you to face the other way."

For a moment my brow scrunches and then I realize… "Oh, you mean sixty-nine."

His brows go up and his mouth presses into a thin line, both his hands tightening on me. "How do you know that?"

"I don't live in a cave." But I'm already turning.

His hands on my hips stop me. "Have you done it before?" His voice is sharp and rough.

Is he jealous? It doesn't scare me at all. In fact, it makes me feel…powerful.

I finish my pivot, my thighs back around his face but now I can run my hands down his abdomen, which I do, before I grab his already leaking cock.

I bend low, skimming my tongue just over the tip to collect that little pearl of liquid on my tongue. "Would it matter?"

And then I swallow, because I love the way he tastes.

He slides a finger inside me, curling it at the tip to push in all the right places as I shift my hips back to bring my seam closer to his mouth. "I just assumed you'd been locked down tight and all this was new."

He sounds…hurt. And I realize I've made a few strides of my own.

Good. "It is new." I lift up so that I peek through our bodies and make eye contact. Because I think we might also need some trust if we're not keeping our hands off each other. "Jess's friends are kind of slutty and they talk…a lot."

He gives me this one-sided grin that makes me crazy. "And they've enlightened you?"

I nod and then settle my belly back down on his chest, sliding my lips around his cock again. I suck him all the way in, nearly down to his base and then slowly pull him out again. "For example, Amanda explained in great detail how you relax your throat." And then I lick him again, sucking him back into my mouth.

"I think I like this Amanda."

I stop, my turn to feel the sharp stab of jealousy of my own as I pop back off. "Then why don't you go kidnap her?"

He gives the heartiest chuckle I've ever heard as he slaps my ass playfully. "Oh sweetheart, you're all the captive I can handle."

Somehow, that makes me feel better. "And why am I all you can handle?"

"In addition to being the sexiest woman I have ever met," those words have my belly fluttering. "You're also gorgeous, sweet, innocent, and you've got my balls fucking aching. So please, baby girl, I'll beg this time, but I need you to suck my dick."

"Is that what you need, Daddy?" My words are said in a husky whisper, but I don't bend back down. Instead, I roll my hips, so that Jake licks me. My head tosses back, it feels so good.

His arms wrap around my hips, lifting me up. "You know I do."

I bend over and sink my mouth down the length of him, taking him all the way in.

He rewards me by sliding three fingers in my aching pussy while he swirls his tongue over my clit.

I slide my mouth back up his shaft, trying to keep from completely falling apart. Taking him in my mouth while he eats me out is even better than what we did earlier and my breath hitches on a little sob as I go to sink back down him.

But his hand, pulling my hair, stops me. "Are you all right, sweetheart? Anything wrong?"

"Nothing," I whisper the words against the head of his cock. "This is just so good, I..."

I don't even know how to finish that sentence, so I sink back down him as he loosens his grip on my hair.

His hand trails down my spine, over my ass.

His tongue starts working my clit again, his fingers pumping in and out of my pussy.

And then with his other hand, he takes his index finger and circles my other hole

It's like fire erupts inside me. I can't get enough. I want every ounce of this man's energy, every drop of his cum.

I sink back down on him taking all of him as he pushes his finger just inside.

I can't take it anymore, and I explode, the orgasm that rocks through me makes me blank out for the barest second as I slide off him, gasping for breath.

"Nia," he begs. "Please, baby."

Blinking my eyes, I take him back in my mouth, just in time for his cock to explode, a stream of cum filling my mouth.

I swallow him down, so satisfied in this moment.

It's not just my orgasm but his that fills me with warmth as I melt into him, collapsing onto his body.

And I can't explain it, but some shift has occurred. I believe him and his promises this time. It feels so good.

My muscles are jelly as Jake lifts me and turns me around, settling me into his side, his arms wrapping about me as my head comes to his shoulder.

"That was..." My voice drifts off, my eyes closing. I feel like I could sleep for a week. I don't even realize I've drifted off to sleep when Jake's voice wakes me.

"Sweetheart. Don't go to sleep yet."

"Why?" Is my sleepy answer. He's so comfortable and I am beyond relaxed. It seems like the perfect moment to sleep.

"Because…" His voice is filled with enough tension that I lift my head. "We need to talk."

CHAPTER TWENTY-ONE

Jake

I know that I'll eventually have to come clean about everything, but now is not the moment.

I need Nia to trust me so that I can turn these next events to her advantage. I've never felt more like I'm threading a needle, but if I play this just right, I can put Toni behind bars, get the right Italians at the head of her family, and pacify mine.

It's a big ask but the plan is starting to form.

I just need her to give me some information that will help me to make all this happen. Is it fair that I need her to tell me everything while I'm withholding several key details?

No. It isn't.

And if I'm not careful, I'm going to lose her because of these choices.

Which is mind-blowing because I never thought I'd want to keep a woman ever in my life, but I want to keep her.

I want to keep her so badly, I fucking ache.

I gather her closer, the way her body fits against mine is like nothing I've felt before. She's so soft and warm, her little sighs are as satisfying as her moans.

And the sex...

Holy fuck. I've been with all types of women. But Nia...she sets me on fire.

"What do we need to talk about?" she whispers. I look down, those blue eyes holding mine, large and filled with worry.

Touching her chin, I bend closer to kiss her lips in a light kiss. "I have news."

"What kind?"

Softly I stroke her cheek. "Your father..."

I feel the tension that skates through her and pull her even closer. "What happened?"

"He set off a bomb—"

"What?!?"

"At the Starlet. He's on camera doing it."

She stares at me, her mouth open. "But that means..."

"He's going to prison, Nia. You'll never see him again if you don't want to."

She shakes her head, rolling away from me and laying on her back on the narrow bed.

She's still naked, one of arms lifting above her head as she stares up at the ceiling. I can't help myself as I lay a light hand on her belly. I just want to keep her close.

Her skin slides like silk under my fingers and my chest aches. "Sweetheart?"

She shakes her head as she squeezes her eyes shut. "You really think your family can prosecute him?"

"Of course," I say, my confidence in the answer pulling my shoulders straight.

"Of course," she repeats and then she looks at me. "Your family has the power my family dreams of."

"And what do you dream of?"

"Getting out," she whispers. "Away from Toni. In a place where I'm safe."

"I can give you that place," I say before I can hold back the words.

She nods. "I was running away. I bought plane tickets and everything. No one is going to think I was stolen."

My stomach dips. "Please believe me, sweetheart. I was never going to hurt you. I'm protecting you and that protection lasts for as long as you choose. Hell. For the rest of your life if you want."

She looks at me then. "You really mean it? Like really, really mean it?"

I push up from the bed then. I was prepared for this moment. Sliding open one of my drawers, I fish for the box I know is at the back.

What I didn't plan for was for this moment to be real. I bought this ring as a ploy. One more way to get Nia to trust me.

It makes me feel like shit that I'm still using this moment to gain her trust. But it's not to hurt her, it's to help her.

I swear…somewhere over the last week, I became this woman's soldier.

I pull out the box, turning back to the bed.

There she lays, still naked, one arm over her head, the swell of her hips and her plump breasts on full display.

I stare at her, just drinking her in. How do I tell her that I'd do almost anything just to get to look at her? Touch her?

Shaking off my thoughts, I walk over with the box in hand, snapping open the lid. Inside is a three-and-a-half-carat near-flawless diamond set in platinum. She is meant for cool tones and this ring is perfect for her.

Her eyes flip down to the ring and then back up to my eyes. "You came prepared."

It's not a compliment. Her voice drops, becoming more guarded.

I lower myself onto my haunches next to the bed. "It was always my plan to give you whatever measure of protection you required."

I know the first part is a lie. But the second…I mean every word.

Her brows lift as she nips at her lip. She turns on her side, her hand propping up her head, her blonde hair spilling down and pooling on the pillow. I reach out to run my fingers through the thick strands, looking to reconnect with her, make this moment what it should be, not filled with guarded worry.

"You think that's a good plan? Tie ourselves together for life?"

I lift the long strands to my own face, inhaling her scent. My feelings are something I'm still figuring out, but I can say this with absolutely certainty, you're the only woman I would ever consider offering for."

"Why is that?"

I swallow. "I mean, besides the fact that you're stunningly gorgeous and so sexy that I can barely see straight?"

A small smile touches her lips. "Besides that."

"We were both forged in the fire. We've both seen real darkness. We understand each other, don't we?"

She nods. "I think we do."

I take the ring out of the box and reach for her hand. Then, I slip the piece on her finger.

She chews on her lip like she's still not sure.

"You can take some time to think. I'll understand if you change your mind. But my family's protection gives you all the options, Nia."

She stares at me, cocking her head.

"And I can make certain Toni Carcetti never steps out of prison."

Her fingers thread into mine. "Is that a promise?"

"Promise," I say bringing her knuckles to my lips.

The ring on her finger catches a bit of moonlight, sparkling in the dim light. It looks so right on her finger, and I climb back into the bed, settling her against my body again.

Her head settles on my chest, her body fitting to mine again. "Jake?"

"Yeah, sweetheart?"

"I've lived a lie for the past ten years. I can't do that with you, you know?"

It's not a lie. Not anymore. My feelings are real and whatever amount of commitment she needs from me, I'm here for it. But it's only as I mull the words, I realize she's not talking about me. "A lie?"

My heart picks up speed, thumping in my chest. "That Toni is your father?"

"That he isn't a monster," she whispers back.

My hands spread out on her body. I need to know what she knows but also, even more than that, I need to protect her. "Tell me."

She takes a deep breath. "I saw him…"

My stomach bottoms out, weighed down like it's been filled with lead. But I don't say a word. This is the moment I've been waiting for. Building toward.

But I care less about knowing the secret for my gain and more about taking this burden from her. I can't imagine how she's carried it alone. "What did you see him do?" I hold her closer, resting my chin on her head.

"I had a nightmare. I couldn't sleep. So I went to her room…"

I squeeze my eyes shut. Fuck. Even hearing it is hard. I hate that she went through all of this. "What did you see, sweetheart?"

"I saw him holding her under the water," her voice breaks on a sob. "I never told anyone. When he saw me, he said he was trying to save her. That's what I told the police."

"You lied for him."

She nods into my chest. "I was so afraid."

"Of course you were, baby." I know what she needs to hear and I'm happy to give it to her. She's alive because she lied. "You did the right thing."

She lifts her head, tears shimmering in her eyes and rolling down her cheeks. "I hate myself for what I didn't do for her. You shouldn't marry me. I can't be trusted. I—"

I pull her on top of me, her body pressed all down the length of mine. "You should never have had to face him alone. Do you understand me? You were a little girl, and he was as big and bad as they come." I hold her face in my hands. "You let me fight him from here on out, do you hear me, Nia? You let me be your weapon."

More tears leak from her lids as she gives the tiniest nod.

"I could never rely on him. He was always the enemy…" she whispers. "Swear to me you're not going to be my enemy too."

Fuck. My heart twists as I look into the bottomless depth of those blue irises. But I'm ready. For the first time in my life, I'm ready to say the words and really mean them. "I promise you that I am here for you. That I will always protect you and not hurt you."

She lays her head on my chest. "Don't trust the Vendettis. Any of them. And the Carcettis aren't much better. But my aunt's kids, the Andrianis. They're who you want to put in charge."

I wrap her deep in my embrace. "Go to sleep, sweetheart. I'll be right here when you wake up."

She falls asleep almost instantly, her body still on top of mine. Reaching down to the floor, I grab my pants without moving her and then pull out my phone.

There must be twenty, thirty messages. I scan them, then send a quick message. *Everything is fine. False alarm.*

Roman instantly answers. *How do I know this is even you?*

One side of my mouth turns down as I stare at the phone. They're worried we were infiltrated. *You've got a scar on your left ass cheek. I put it there.*

Okay, that's you. Roman sends the text but then three more bubbles appear. *I still think it's time for a face-to-face meeting. Things are getting really hot.*

Normally, I'd be happy to see Roman. He's always a voice of reason. But what's happening between me and Nia is far mor personal than I ever intended and I'm not sure I can explain.

I don't answer as I set the phone down and close my eyes.

It's time for me to get some sleep. With a few hours under my belt, I'll be able to fully form this plan. The one that helps my family and keeps Nia safe.

Because, choosing between them is not an option.

CHAPTER TWENTY-TWO

Nia

I wake up still completely on top of Jake. It never occurred to me that a person might sleep on top of another person, but there is a lot about desire and intimacy I am learning.

I told him my deepest, darkest secret last night and my worst fear…

And here I am, still in his arms.

I knew I would lose this war, but I'm not even sure what I was fighting. Why was I fighting?

His strength is holding me up and taking my burdens one by one. I lay my head back down on his chest, my hair spilling over his collarbone and shoulder.

"You're awake," he rumbles, I feel it on my cheek.

"Sorry if I woke you."

"Not at all," he murmurs low, combing his fingers through my hair. "I'm glad you did. I like being up with you."

"Who said anything about getting up," I sigh rubbing my cheek through his chest hair. "I say we stay right here."

He chuckles as he lifts my hand, now sporting a very large diamond, bringing my palm to his lips. "I like that plan."

I look at the ring sparkling on my finger, my eyes going wide.

In the dark I had no idea it was so stunning. It's ridiculously big and the sparkle is off the charts.

My lips part as I stare. This is the kind of ring Jess and her friends would froth over.

Jess.

My breath hitches. "Jake?"

"What?" I feel him tense under me.

"If Toni is going to prison, where is my sister?" My eyes lift to meet his.

He picks up his phone from nightstand as he types in what can I only assume is a text. "I'll find out," he answers.

He stares at the screen, waiting for a response and then types something back.

I haven't seen any electronics since we arrive, and for a moment, I look at it blankly, knowing I should be plotting to get that phone. This is the moment I've been waiting for.

And yet, I don't care. I don't want to leave. I think I've made my decision. I'll stay, and let Jake's very large shadow protect me. And I'll try to heal those wounds I've been carrying for so long instead of running from them.

I never wanted to trust a man with my heart but for the first time in actual years, I'm ready to give myself to someone else. Him.

I take a breath, folding my hands on his chest.

"Jess is fine," he answers.

"How do you know?"

"The guard who let you out..." He winces as I lift my head.

"The one she was blowing?"

His brows lift. "No wonder he was so quick to act," he mutters, with a shake of his head. "Anyway. The moment Toni set off that bomb, Mike left with her."

My eyes go wide. "Wait. She got kidnapped too?"

Jake shakes his head. "Kidnapped? He's my cousin and not actually a guard, though he is in security directly under my leadership. And while he's not one of the five shareholders, he does very well as the head of security for the Kincaid casinos. You tell me how much convincing your sister needed."

A smile breaks out on my face. "You're telling me that my sister is also being protected by a Kincaid?"

"Well, technically his name is Mike Brody. But yes, she's under Kincaid protection. Like I said, we don't hurt women."

I surge forward, kissing his lips hard and fast because it's more than I ever imagined. In my perfect world, I'd have my sister and my scumbag father would be in prison.

My legs naturally fall to either side of his, cradling his hips as my fingers twine into his hair.

I don't even know how to thank him, but I do know a few things I want to do to show my affection.

His hands come to my ass, taking both cheeks in his hands and squeezing, pulling me tighter into his already rock-hard cock.

There is no part of me that wants to hold back in this moment, and I rock into him, the head of his cock slipping through my still wet folds.

We both groan because this time the press of his head doesn't hurt like it did yesterday. Not that I'm worried about the pain.

I want to be Jake's and I don't care how much it costs.

But he's still got his hands on my ass, and he stops me from taking more of him. "Are you sure, baby?"

"I'm sure," I whisper against his lips. "So sure."

"Nice and slow then. We don't want to hurt you." And then he slowly loosens his grip allowing me to slowly sink down on him.

It burns, his hardness almost shocking as he fills me. But I also feel so connected to him in this moment. Like we're joined together in a way that can't be broken apart.

I let out a breath that sounds a bit like a cry.

He instantly stills, his hands cradling my hips.

"It's all right," I say, lifting up just high enough to look him in the eye. "I'm not hurt. I just..."

"What, baby?"

"It just feels really emotional. I've needed you for so long."

He kisses me then. Long and slow and soft. It makes my eyes prick with tears.

"I've needed you too, Nia. We were meant to be here, meant to be together."

I don't say anything, but I feel everything. The rightness of those words, the strength in his body, the fullness of him being inside me.

It's wonderful, and frightening, and fulfilling.

The stretching and burning crests as he completely fills me. My clit presses to his pubic bone, the first bit of pleasure dulling the pain and my eyes go wide. "Oh."

He gives me that grin. The one that pulls at one side of his mouth, making him look sexy, and mysterious, and a little dangerous.

Then he pulls my hips up so that he's sliding out of me before he pushes slowly back in.

With each thrust the pain recedes, the pleasure building until I'm pushing down on him, chasing pleasure that's even deeper and fuller than what he gave last night.

He finally releases my hips and instead twines our fingers together, joining our hands, our bodies moving to a shared rhythm that steals my words, my breath.

The only thing I can feel is him.

I'm making these noises…evolving from mewls of pain to pleasure as they turn into moans.

He thrusts harder, stronger up into me, as I climb. "Oh God," I moan, finally making words. "That's so…"

"You like that?" he grunts before he takes my mouth in a fierce kiss, our tongues tangling together.

The kiss only makes the pleasure more intense, my body tightening as an orgasm threatens to pull me under.

I try to hold out. I've waited for this moment for so long, but the pleasure grows so intense, everything pulls as tight as a drum and then I break, the first crashing wave of pleasure washing over me.

I cry out, my body spasming around his thick length.

Which sets off his finish, his chorus of groans joining mine.

He keeps pumping in and out of me, even as the orgasms finish, our muscles relaxing into each other.

Our hands are joined, our arms touching. Chest to chest, hip to hip, he kisses me again.

It feels like we're completely tangled up, our bodies like some elaborate knot, too tied together to ever come apart.

We stay like that for a long time, neither wanting to break the contact until Jake finally slides his hands from mine. "What do you say I put you in the shower while I make you coffee?"

It sounds like heaven. "I've got a better idea. What if we first shower and then coffee?"

"Together?" His lips tug into a smile again. "I like it."

He's up with me in his arms, carrying me into the bathroom. Lightly he sets me on my feet and then pulls back the curtain. "All clear."

I laugh a little, kind of loving that we have this routine where he checks the shower for me. It feels personal in this small way that he's looking out for me. "Thank you."

He turns on the water, putting his hand in to check the temperature and then he reaches for my hand, helping me over the lip.

The warm spray hits my body and I groan at how good it feels. He gives my hand a squeeze as he steps in too.

Reaching for the soap, he lathers his hands and then works the suds all over my body, until my skin is shiny clean and I'm ready to get it dirty again.

But he only chuckles into my hair. "Let's give you a bit of a rest, no?"

It feels a bit like a rejection and my lip juts out. He nips at it with his teeth a moment before he straightens up. "Don't be hurt, sweetheart. Trust me when I say, I'm abstaining for your benefit." And then he points down at his cock.

I laugh because, yeah, he's clearly ready. I take the soap in hand and lather my palms up too, a moment before I run one wet slippery hand down his chest, over his rippling abdominal muscles and through the dark swath of hair above his cock before I slide my hand down the long, thick length of him.

His teeth grit together. "Don't ask me how I could be this hard after what we just did."

"I like it," I whisper, pumping his raging erection in my small hand. His much-larger hand covers mine, helping me as he wraps his other arm around my body, cupping my ass to pull me close.

"It's going to take me a long time to get enough of you."

"I hope so. I'm thinking about taking you up on your offer."

His hand pauses, making mine pause too. "Marriage?"

I give a little nod before he kisses me, his hand moving again, up and down his cock. It only takes four, five more pumps and he's cumming.

I still love seeing it, my gaze glued to him as his cum spills on the shower floor and then washes away.

Wrapping me in his arms, he gives me a long tender hug. Then he grabs the soap and finishes the washing I was supposed to give him. "You take your time," he says as he rinses off. "I'm going to make you that coffee."

I nod as he steps out of the shower. I'm mostly done, so with a final rinse off, I step out too.

Wrapping myself in a towel, I blow out my hair and then put on a bit of makeup. I know it's just me and Jake but today…I agreed to be his wife.

A pulse of warm energy rushes through me. I can't believe it!

Still in just a towel, I make my way into the bedroom to dress.

"Your coffee's ready," he calls from the kitchen.

"Be right there," I answer, opening a drawer to pull out underwear and a bra.

Reaching in the closet for a dress, I step into the silky fabric and zip it up. Just as I finish, I hear a ding.

His phone is on the nightstand.

Looking over, I pick it up to bring it to him, but the message makes me stop. It's from Roman…

. . .

It's time to finish this and dump the girl, Jake. She'll be the Carcettis' problem to toss or clean up.

CHAPTER TWENTY-THREE

NIA

I STARE AT THE SCREEN, the words turning my stomach as I stare.

It's all been a lie…

A broken noise escapes my lips and I cover my mouth with my hand. He can't hear me, because I need time to think.

I try to open the phone and see the other messages but, of course, I don't know the code.

"Nia," Jake calls. "Your cappuccino is getting cold."

My chin jerks up. I lived a lie for years, but with Jake, I'm so wide open, one look at my face and he'll know something is wrong.

Then again, I don't know how we avoid this one.

He made me promises.

I sob into my hand, my knees giving out so that I sink onto the bed. The one on which I just lost my virginity.

My nails dig into my face as I squeeze my eyes shut, the emotion threatens to burst out of me.

All those promises…it's obvious that he didn't mean them. How could I be so stupid? A silly little virgin so ready to believe that he loved me. But he was planning on dumping me all along…

All at once, I wonder what that might mean.

Is it drop me at the airport? In the desert?

Is Jake going to hurt me?

My blood runs cold. It's not like I haven't experienced a man who I thought loved me deciding I was the enemy.

A wave of grief so strong hits me as I fold my head between my knees, tears leaking out of my eyes. I swipe at the water, mascara and eyeliner smearing on my hand. What a stupid, stupid girl I am.

Another sob rises up in my chest, but I swallow it back down. I was made for this.

I don't cry. I don't openly grieve. I just soldier on.

I squeeze my eyes shut, muffling my scream in my leg. What is it about having some hope that makes it harder to live in the darkness of despair?

I suddenly don't want to do this anymore.

I remember that promise that I asked Jake to make. That he'd kill me rather than give me back to Toni.

He didn't make it. He said he would never hurt me, and he wasn't giving me back.

"Nia. Your coffee." He's in the door and I clutch the phone to my chest, still bent in half, I keep my head down, like he won't know somethings wrong if he doesn't see my face.

"Is everything all right?"

"Fine," I force my voice to remain even, but I don't look at him. I can't. I sink into myself, trying to decide what to do. Confront him? Pretend?

He comes into the room and passes by me. My head automatically lifts to take in the details of his body. He's shirtless, muscles rippling, and something deep inside me aches.

It's almost pathetic how much I want to curl into him, even now.

He sets the frothy coffee on the nightstand and turns to me. "Why is your head between your knees?"

I stare at the floor, trying to come up with an answer.

"Nia?"

I shake my head, my throat closing on a lump. I can't do what I did with Toni. I can't shut down my emotional side. I just gave Jake my virginity.

I think I might love this man.

The man who's going to dump me and leave me for Toni to clean up. God, I'm so fucking stupid. This is why I knew I shouldn't accept his protection. I was better off alone.

I don't even speak as I hand him his phone. Our fingers brush, though I try to ignore the jolt of electricity that passes through me, as I sit up. I still don't look at him. I can't.

He takes the phone but doesn't even look at the screen. Instead, he's sinking down in front of me, balancing on the balls of his feet, resting his elbows on his knees. "Are you regretting what we just did?"

A wild laugh bubbles up my chest. Regret doesn't even begin to touch what I feel. "Regret?" I shake my head, steal suddenly stiffening my spine. "That's one word..."

"Tell me what's going on."

"You really are just like my daddy," the last word comes out as a sneer.

His brow scrunches. "I don't know what you mean by that."

"A gangster. Ready to throw me away when I'm not convenient anymore." The words sound far away, like someone else is speaking them.

"I promised to marry you."

"Lie," I push out on a half sob. "It's a lie, isn't it?"

His mouth purses into a line, his eyes wincing with regret.

I push up, spinning and darting past him. I don't know where I think I'm going, there is nowhere to go.

But there is more space in the living room and kitchen, and I run out there, stopping in the space where the kitchen ends and the living room begins.

He's right behind me and I spin to...I don't even know...scream, fight, cry. He hooks my waist and pulls me close.

I don't melt into him, but I can't deny that as his scent fills my nostrils, I want to. How crazy that the very man who is going to end me is the one I want to protect me. "I hate you," I whisper into his chest.

"Why? Tell me. What happened?"

He methodically planned, so I know he knows I saw something on his phone. He's far too smart to not have made the connection. "Why don't you look?"

"Because," he lets out a long breath, his hand coming to the back of my head. "I want you to tell me."

I stand there, his body pressed to mine, one hand on the small of my back, one in my hair. I don't lean my body against his, but I do put the weight of my skull in his hand, tipping my head back to look into his eyes.

God, his eyes are this gray that's like the sea during a storm. They've always captivated me, held me hostage, and I pause now, lips parting as my heart does that flip it always does when my gaze meets his.

"Are you really going to marry me or is that just some sick joke?"

His eyes widen in a way that makes him look guilty. "What are you talking about?"

But I don't answer as a strange sound catches my ear. We've been in the middle of nowhere for days and I didn't even notice that there was no car noise, no engines running, no sounds other than the nature around us.

My head cocks as I listen.

"Fuck," he rumbles, but his hands don't leave me, if anything they tighten. "It's a chopper."

"Helicopter?" I look back at him, fear making my thoughts slow. "Who?"

"I'm not sure," he steps back then but he takes my hand, pulling me with him. "Put on jeans and a T-shirt. Something sturdy. Drink your coffee. We'll talk as soon as I figure out what's going on but do not, for one second, think that we are not getting married. We are. I meant every promise I made."

I don't even know what to do with that. His family would say he's lying. And their message chain clearly states they intend to dump me.

But I do what he says, because he's right. Whatever's coming, I'll do better if I'm not in a dress.

I wiggle myself into jeans as Jake puts on a shirt and I hear him rumble behind me.

"What?" I turn, worried, he's seen something, but his eyes are on me.

"I've never seen you in jeans before."

"So?"

His gaze is dark, the heat in it making my breath catch for a different reason. I should not allow him to distract me. He isn't what he promised he'd be, that heat is a lie.

The sound of the helicopter is getting louder. Pulling on his workout sneakers, I tug a white T-shirt over my head just in time for him to kiss my forehead. "Whatever you're thinking, don't. Whoever is in that chopper, I will keep you safe."

And then he's gone.

I want to believe him. I do. But as I trail behind him back out of the bedroom, I know I shouldn't. I've learned the truth…

From the bank of windows in the living room, I see the helicopter land in the hardpack desert sand.

I feel myself tense, but his shoulders relax. "Don't worry," his deep voice reverberates through me. "It's just Roman."

But the name slices at my gut.

Roman.

I know why he's here.

Jake swipes his finger over the keypad, stepping outside, and leaving the door partially ajar as he strides to the chopper.

I see a tall, dark-haired man in sunglasses and an impeccably cut suit step out of the helicopter, ducking as he moves to meet Jake.

While Jake makes me feel at home, this man has me tensing after the text I read…

I spin, needing some water or something to calm my racing heart when I see them…

The keys on counter, a little H emblem on the key fob. The Honda keys and my ticket out of here...

Snatching up the keys, I start for the open door. I've only ever driven twice, my cousin taking me around a parking lot.

Toni never taught us; Jess and I were always driven by a chauffeur. It sounds luxurious, but it's one more way he kept control.

I hope I remember how as I start for the door.

I planned to teach myself in Canada, when I'd purchased a car. But this is so different. Jake will see me leave, he'll follow...

Opening it only a tiny bit more, I slip out and then move to the side of the house.

Jake and Roman are talking.

Roman's got his hands crossed over his chest, while Jake's fists are clenched at his sides. I can't see Jake's face, but Roman looks pissed.

I could go back inside. Assume Jake's fighting for me.

But is that a chance I really want to take? I've been stupidly naïve and it's time I take some control.

Crouching down, I hit the button to unlock the car, watching to see if they notice. They're yelling now.

Roman takes out his phone, pointing at the screen.

Jake pulls his from his pocket too, swiping over the screen. Then he gives Roman a good hard push.

This is my moment...

I creep out, staying down and climb into the car on the passenger's side. Crawling over the console, I slide into the driver's seat.

For a moment, I close my eyes, trying to remember my cousin's lessons.

Push the brake, hit the start button.

The car turns over, coming to life. With a surge of triumph, I press the D button and let my foot off the brake and the car lurches forward.

I give a little scream as I grip the wheel in both hands and hit the gas...

CHAPTER TWENTY-FOUR

JAKE

EVEN OVER THE CHOPPER, I hear the change in vibration of another engine starting.

I look over my shoulder in time to see the taillights of the Accord turn off and the car jolt forward.

"What the fuck?"

And that's the moment that Nia glances back at me from the driver's seat. She looks scared out of her mind, her big eyes even wider and her lips parted as the car moves.

"Stop," I rumble, taking a step in her direction but she shakes her head, and I know, she's running again. Who can blame her?

"Seatbelt!" I bellow over all the noise, making a gesture with my hand as I spring toward her.

I watch her click in and for a moment, relief washes through me. But gripping the wheel she hits the gas and takes off.

The car swerves this way and that, like Nia has no idea how to steer. My heart jumps into my throat as I stare for another second before I pivot back to Roman. "We have to catch her."

"No," Roman answers. "Let her go."

I finish my turn back to him and, without warning, swing my fist, clocking him a good one in the jaw. Fucker deserves it.

And right now, I'm not playing.

Roman, Mason, Leo. They are tough men. I won't deny it. But none of them have done what I had to, none of them have my grit. It's a fact that they all know, but Roman is getting a solid reminder lesson.

He reels back, closer to the chopper, and grabbing him by the collar, I bend him down below the blades and push him toward the door.

We are not going to stand here and argue, we are going after Nia, and I don't have time or patience to explain.

But he recovers before I can shove him into the bird and hits me with a good gut shot that has me doubling over. I let him go with a push to the side and jump in the helicopter myself. "Follow that car," I bark at the pilot, Carl.

Carl knows every Kincaid, he's been with the family for a long time, and he knows that Roman and I are equals, at best.

As the actual patriarch of this family, I'm being generous.

Roman jumps in just before the chopper lifts off the ground. "You were going to leave me?"

"At a fully stocked house," I answer back, pulling the protective headphones over my ears that are also equipped with microphones so we can better hear each other. He pulls his on too. "Yes. I was going to leave you. And you fucking deserve it."

"I meant what I said this morning. Let her go. It's the easiest way for this whole thing to go away. We don't need her anymore."

"I need her," I answer back, knowing what I'm revealing. "And I'm not letting her go, so you can either help or get the fuck out of my way."

"Jake. You're not thinking straight."

I glare at him. "I'm thinking the same about you. I don't know what's twisted in your brain, but I know what kind of man you are. I was there when you moved heaven and earth to help Charlotte."

"Charlotte was innocent."

"Nia is innocent," I fire back, done with this conversation. "You don't know shit."

"She's Toni's daughter. Of course she's not innocent."

"Wrong on both counts. Like I said. You don't know shit." I turn to the open door of the chopper, watching the Accord careen down the road, bouncing from side to side. She's driving way too fast, and she doesn't seem to have control of the car.

My heart is pounding as I watch the car bounce over a rock, nearly running off the road. "Baby girl," I'm talking to myself now. "Slow down, sweetheart. You're going to get hurt." I can hear the fear in my own voice.

The tarred road is coming up and while I'll be glad to see her on a real surface, and not bouncing all over the rocky desert ground, she's coming into the turn way too fast.

And worse, another car catches my gaze coming down the road toward Nia. Is it my imagination or are they on a crash course?

My fists pound on my thighs a roar rumbling from my lips. "Nia," I grit out. "Please."

"You love her," Roman states quietly, watching the car too.

"She's been a victim this whole time," I answer back, not touching the L-word. "And she's still done nothing but help us."

"How has she helped us?"

I glare at him for a split second before my eyes return to the car. "I'll tell you after I know she's all right."

But the Accord is even less stable than a moment before.

And the car that's coming…a state trooper.

A snarl rips from my throat.

She hits the tar, not even coming close to making the turn.

She does pump the brakes, the car slowing. The trooper swerves and she shoots off the other side of the road, bouncing wildly until the sedan jolts to a stop in some shrub brush.

I see the airbag deploy and another snarl rips from my lips.

And then nothing.

Nia doesn't open the door. She doesn't even move as the chopper does a circle. "Land," I bark at Carl.

"How are you going to explain what just happened to the troopers?" Roman asks me.

"You're a smart kid," I answer back. "Think of something. Fast."

"Christ," Roman growls out on a frustrated breath. "You're serious?"

But he doesn't say anything else as the bird hits the ground and I spring from my seat, racing toward the car.

I wrench the door open, Nia is so still I stop, my breath sticking in my chest.

"Ow," she moans as her head turns toward me. "That hurt."

"Nia." I'm down on my haunches, unbuckling her seatbelt. "You scared me so much."

My eyes are scanning her body. My breath rushes out, she looks... unharmed. Nothing broken, no blood.

"Not as much as you scared me."

My stomach clenches as I go to pull her out of the car.

"Stop," one of the troopers commands. My teeth gnash but I obey. "You can't move her in case she's injured."

Roman steps up next to me. "I was just explaining to the officers that we saw the car from the chopper while we were surveying our land," Roman gives the officers a large smile.

"My wife was attempting to teach herself to drive," I add, not even looking at the troopers. They will not deny me access to her, not now, and not at the hospital because I know that's where we're headed next.

My ring still glints on her finger.

I brush Nia's blonde hair back from her cheek as her eyes slide closed. "Hey," I say, her eyes opening back up. "No falling asleep now."

She blinks at me slowly. "I'm not a good driver."

"No shit," Roman murmurs.

"You can say it," she ignores Roman. "I don't have the skill to get myself out of any of this do I? I'm at your mercy. At his."

"No," I shake my head. "I told you. I will—"

"I'm going to need you to make that promise now," she whispers to me.

I instantly know what she's talking about. "I don't want to promise that, because it's not going to come to anything like that. I meant every word I said."

"Promise anyway."

"If I'm going to betray you," I say, "then my word doesn't mean anything anyway."

"What is she saying," one of the officers asks.

Roman steps between them and us. "Gibberish. My uncle is just keeping her talking. Concussion probably. How long until the ambulance arrives?"

"Nia," I say just loud enough for her and Roman to hear. "I am not going to hurt you for any reason."

"No. Promise. Promise you'll end me before you give me back. I have to know it won't be his way." She lets out a sob. "Promise. Please."

I know she needs to hear the words. Some men might lie. Others might be willing to really do it. But I could never hurt her and I'll never hide the truth from her again. "I made you a different promise, remember? I'll die before I let him hurt you. I swear, I meant it, Nia. Every word."

Her eyes go wide.

Roman gives a loud cough to cover our conversation but I see him shift, his gaze flitting back to her. "I'm beginning to understand," he says to me.

"About fucking time," I rumble back, stroking her cheek as her head lulls back, her eyes fluttering closed again.

"No sleeping," my light strokes turn into a pat. "You need to stay right here with me."

Her eyes fix on mine again. But they're dilated, the pupils so big, I mutter a string of curses under my breath.

In the distance, I hear the sirens as I give her arm a vigorous rub. "Nia, baby girl, want to hear another story?"

Her eyes open again. "Story?"

"Yeah. This one is about Mason and Leo."

"Mason and Leo," she lifts her head. "Your nephews?"

"That's right. They love each other, but they fight like two bickering old women. Always have. Mason thinks he knows everything, and Leo has always run hot under the collar."

Her eyes are focusing on me, and I reach for her hand and slide her fingers into mine. "Me and Jess are a little like that. So different. But I love her."

I want to pull her out of the car so badly, take her in my arms. "That's exactly right. So the two of them fought all time. But then it changed."

I'm just trying to keep her talking. Keep her engaged. "What?"

"I told you, Leo was with my brother when it happened."

She nods, the tiniest little jerk of her chin.

"And he went from hot to..."

"Batshit crazy," Roman offers as the ambulance pulls off the road, the two officers going to meet it.

"That's about right. And in his crazy, he nearly detonated us all. He was hard, and angry, and he forgot how to think with his heart. He almost really hurt Mason and Charlotte, Mason's wife."

"Leo did that?" she asks, but her eyes are getting unfocused again.

I grip her hand tighter. "He did and I thought for sure we were going to lose him."

"What happened?"

"He found Kim," I answer, bringing the back of her fingers to my lips. "And she taught him how to love again, reminded him of the man he was always supposed to be. Brought him back from the darkness."

"The man he was supposed to be..." she whispers, and I see her fading again. I give her arm a little shake.

"The man who protects the people around him. Just like I'm going to protect you."

But her eyes close again.

"Nia," I bark loud enough for her eyes to flutter open before they start to close again.

But she can't close her eyes. Not now. My heart is thundering in my ears. "Wake up." She has to be all right. Because I've finally admitted to myself that I love her....

CHAPTER TWENTY-FIVE

Nia

A steady beeping is the first thing I hear.

I slide my eyes open, looking to the side. A heart-rate monitor fills my vision. My hand creeps out, touching hard plastic bed rails on the side of the bed. I'm in the hospital.

I turn my head the other way, the room coming into view.

The large door to the hall is closed. A sink sits to one side, some cabinets. Another door that I assume leads to the bathroom is opposite the sink. It's like every hospital I've ever been in with beige walls, white plastic and pale pink accents.

I try to lift my head, but it aches, and I close my eyes against the pain.

How did I get here?

Memories of the car, of trying to escape float through my thoughts. Fragmented edges of the helicopter and the car skidding across the road are next and I flex my hands, trying to clear my head. Is that how I ended up here?

I remember Jake next to the car. Remember him holding my hand and murmuring softly. I can't recall the words, but I remember the feeling. He was so tender…

Which seems odd. I ran away. He was going to get rid of me…

A few phrases rise to the surface of my thoughts. *Better man, love, the man he was supposed to be...*

"Finally awake, princess?" A voice speaks from the shadowed corner of the room but my blood turns to ice in my veins. Because that's not Jake.

It's Toni.

I gasp in fear. which makes my head throb painfully. I reach my hands up, holding my head. Why is Toni here? Cold dread makes my body recoil in pain. "Where am I?"

"Don't you know?" His voice is hard as ever, not an ounce of softness tinging its edges.

I shake my head, not sure what to do. Think, Nia. Think. "I…I was in a car. I tried to drive…"

"Where were you driving to?"

Shit. More of Jake's words filter through my thoughts. His promise to die before he let Toni hurt me reverberates in my head. Where is he? Where is Jake?

I've lied to Toni for years and the words slip from my lips now. Not that I'm lying exactly, but I need to be very careful about what I say.

I wish my head were clearer. I swipe my fingers across my forehead. "Away."

"Away?" I hear his snort. He doesn't believe me.

"I…" I swallow. I could tell Toni the truth. I was kidnapped against my will. Held. But it's a lie too. Because I'd stay with Jake if I thought he truly wanted to keep me.

"That's a nice ring on your finger, princess. Is that the price for betraying me?"

My mouth drops open as I lift my head, dropping my hand. I see Jake's ring still sparkling on my finger, catching even the smallest bit of light. It's some reminder that for a moment, I had real hope. That I saw another life that didn't involve Toni. And in that life, I wasn't alone.

I'm done pretending with this man and I'm done living in fear. He breaks everything that's close to him and I know I'm next. But I can't bring myself to care. "I betrayed you? That's hilarious."

He pushes up from the chair. "Stupid bitch. Probably thinking with what's between your legs just like your whore of a mother. She deserved to die, and you deserve it too."

"Bastard."

"I watched her last breath as I held her under that water and I'll watch yours too," he snarls, stepping up next to the bed.

I lay my head back down, closing my eyes. I can't fight. Only say my piece before the end. It's a calm I never expected to experience. "I saw what you did to her that night, and I told the Kincaids about how you drowned my mother in the bath. You'll rot in prison and then you'll rot in hell."

He yanks the pillow from under my head, my head thumping down on the mattress as pain reverberates through my skull, radiating down my spine.

Then he holds it over my face. "You'll die just like her. I'd tell you all about how she had no loyalty either but we're short on time." He starts to lower the pillow. "I always knew it would come to this."

I close my eyes. I did too.

"Toni," Jake's deep gravelly voice causes my eyes to spring open. I lift my head to see him filling the doorway. "I'm sure you already know, pillows, like the one you're conveniently holding, make excellent silencers."

I gasp in a breath at the sight of a pistol in his hand, even as he steps into the room, raising the gun higher. "Jake," I say, it comes out like a plea.

Despite all our talk about Toni, I never actually pictured this moment, the two men facing off in front of me. I swallow, the numb calmness of the last moments washing away as fear pumps through my veins.

Because I'm scared for Jake.

There isn't an ounce of fear on his face. Jake doesn't look at me, instead his gaze is fixed on Toni, his features drawn into hard lines. My father promptly drops the pillow, pulling his own pistol from his waistband. "If I'm dying, you are too, Kincaid."

"The police are right outside the door," Jake answers evenly. "Fire knowing that you'll never leave this room."

I see Toni wince.

But Jake isn't done. "In one minute, several state troopers are going to arrest you. You're done, Toni. This is the end."

"Arresting me? On what charge? Your stupid brother?"

"No, not yet, You'll go to prison for him. But the arrest, the first charges, will be for Nia."

I cover my mouth to keep from crying out. Because this is everything he promised.

Toni's lip curls. "Do you think you love her? Is that what this is?"

Jake doesn't answer.

"I think I hate you," Toni spits. Jake keeps moving closer, but I see the telltale signs Toni is losing his cool.

His face turns red, his eyes bulging out as he starts around the bed.

"Don't mix up the mind-blowing sex for real love. It isn't. Trust a man who's made that mistake. That's what you'll think it is, and then she'll give her shit away all over town," Toni scoffs.

I gasp at the words. But Jake only gives him a cold smile. "If I were a betting man, I'd say Maria cheated because you were a shit husband."

Toni roars, lunging wildly toward Jake.

But Jake is ready. As Toni leans in, Jake knocks him square in the jaw with a solid punch.

I cry out, my hands twisting into the sheets.

Toni goes down like a wall of brinks hit by a sledgehammer, the noise when he hits the ground deafening. I jump, my head throbbing.

Jake's free hand comes to my arm, gently touching me. "Be still, love. You'll hurt yourself."

"Where were you?" I gasp, gripping his hand in mine. It's not a fair question. I literally crashed his car trying to run away.

"I'm sorry, sweetheart," he answers, grimacing. He keeps his eyes on Toni as the door opens again and several officers stream in. "I got called out to the hall by police to file a report on the accident and Toni took advantage of that moment of distraction."

"What's this?" One of the officers demands from the open doorway.

"I'll explain after you've got him in cuffs," Jake narrows his eyes at the office, offering no explanation.

"I already told you," the officer starts, "we're not making an arrest—"

The room, which had been empty moments ago, fills with more people as Roman and another man, who looks a lot like Jake and Roman, walk into the room.

Behind them, an entire team of men in suits.

Another man in a medical coat that I'm sure is my doctor, enters too. "What is happening here?"

He's quickly pulled from the room by one of the suits as the officers crouch around Toni. "I heard what your lawyer said, but we can't arrest an unconscious man," one grumbles.

"Jake?" Roman asks, his brows up. Without his sunglasses, I can see that Roman has the most classically handsome features of the family. He doesn't look at me, and I grimace at him. I'm not sure I want him here after everything that happened.

The man next to him wears a sardonic grin that makes him look devilish. "Hey, Nia, I'm Luke."

I give him a quick nod, my eyes wary, as I reach for Jake's hand. I need to touch him. I have no idea where we stand, what his motives are, but I'm too hurt, too alone not to cling to the lifeline and hope that is what Jake really is. He did just save my life…

"He had a pillow over Nia's face," Jake answers the officer, not Roman, as he laced his fingers through mine. "I was being generous by punching him."

One of the officers stands. "Is this true?" he asks me, and I nod. Because it is and because Toni deserves everything he's about to get.

Another police officer stands, speaking softly. "Heard the whole thing…multiple charges."

But I hear the first officer mutter back under his breath. "This is a weird one."

Tell me about it, buddy.

I lift Jake's hand and bring it to my cheek. "I'm sorry I took the car." I don't know what else to say. I wish I'd stayed and listened. I wouldn't have been in any more danger than the last several hours have brought.

He leans down, brushing a kiss along my head. From here, I can see the pistol is now tucked into the waistband of his jeans.

I'm not scared, not even a little.

The doctor reenters, looking very annoyed. "We're discharging you to another doctor's care," he says with an irritated frown before he turns and walks back out the door.

Another man comes to the end of my bed to look at the chart, scanning over the information. "We'll set everything up at the compound for her medical needs." This he directs to Jake, his gaze barely touching me.

The suits have all gathered around Toni and are speaking to the police. "Who are they?"

"Lawyers," Jake answers. "Don't worry about them."

"And what about Toni?"

"As soon as he comes to, he'll be taken to prison."

I peek over the side of the bed. He's starting to move.

"And you?"

"I go where you go," he answers, touching my cheek with feather-light fingers. It's the kind of touch that might make a woman melt. I lean into it, closing my eyes. Because that sounds wonderful to me.

I know we have some hard conversations ahead. What were his original plans? Is this ring on my finger all a lie?

Where do we go from here?

But I don't care about the answers just this moment. What I want to do is be tucked into Jake's protection and let the rest of the world melt away.

Toni is carted out on a stretcher, the officers trailing behind. I watch him go, truly hoping to never see him again.

Toni Carcetti is a book I'd very much like to close forever. But what you want and what you get very rarely match.

CHAPTER TWENTY-SIX

Nia

It takes a few hours to leave the hospital, but after that, I'm loaded into the helicopter, the doctor joining Luke, Roman, and Jake as we lift off.

I have no idea where we're going…again.

But this time, I'm not scared. I sink into Jake's side, closing my eyes. I had no choice but to wear the jeans I'd had on this morning, but they're covered in dust and grime, my shirt too.

"As soon as we get you to the house, you can take a hot shower. We'll get your clothes tomorrow, promise."

I nod, not really caring. Just as long as he sleeps with his arms around me, I'll be fine. I close my eyes and burrow into his side.

I know there is still so much unsaid, and I have no idea what will happen after. Which is why I don't speak at all. Just close my eyes and breathe in his scent.

His arm is tight around me, his nose in my hair. I spread my fingers out on his chest, letting my hair cascade over my shoulder.

It's over. Toni's in prison, or he will be soon. I never have to live in fear of him again.

"Here," I hear one of the other men say.

A soft cloth touches my face and I jerk my eyes open, stiffening. It doesn't smell like Jake and my eyes flick down to a handkerchief before I look back up at Jake's face.

"It's Roman's," he says, kissing my forehead. "For your tears."

I didn't even realize I'd been crying. I swipe at my eyes, averting my face so the other men can't see. I don't know them, I don't trust them—Roman in particular—and I don't want to show them any weakness.

But facing Toni...it's stripped me raw. Or maybe it was staring into that pillow and being so certain that was the end.

Jake hugs me tighter, pressing the soft square into my hand. I swipe at the tears some more, even as a soft sob breaks from my lips. "Shit."

"It's all right," Jake nuzzles my ear. "You've earned a good cry."

I shake my head. "No. Not yet. Not here. I..." I don't know how to explain...I feel safe in his arms but that's a very small bubble of space and everything beyond...

I draw in a steadying breath, trying to push the feelings back down. "I'll be all right in a minute. I just need..." This time, I feel the next tear slip down my face.

Jake reaches up with the pad of his thumb and brushes it away.

My eyes close again as I fight for control. I know I'm going to have to fight these men, they want to throw me back to the wolves, and by wolves, I mean my family. And despite the promises Jake has made, I have no idea how this will all shake out.

I need to be strong.

But the tears keep spilling out of my eyes.

Finally, I take the wad of handkerchief in my hand and just cover my face.

If Toni has taught me one thing, it's not to show weakness, and I'm failing right now.

None of the men say a word as Jake pulls me into his lap as another sob breaks from my lips.

I bury my cheek into his shoulder, but I know they can hear me, we're all mic'd. Another sob breaks from my throat, my hands fisting into Jake's shirt.

Jake's hands are spread out over my back, his arms tight around me as the dam I've been trying to keep strong breaks, the cracks that have been collecting finally too much, and a torrent of tears unleash on his shirt.

I push the mic away from my mouth as a feral cry rips from my lips, but I think they hear because one of them says, "Fuck me," into the earpiece.

And the other. "Jesus Christ."

I can't tell who is who, and I'm sure I'm making them wildly uncomfortable, but I just can't hold in the feelings.

I'm crying for my mother, for me, for the past several years... The grief pours out of me in wave after wave as I curl into Jake's embrace, trying to draw from his strength, because without his arms, I'd be a puddle on the floor.

But he never lets me go, and at some point, I hear the words he's been whispering as he holds me. *Brave. Strong. Beautiful.*

The tears finally subside, the sobs receding, but I don't move, I just stay buried in his embrace.

I don't want to face the other men, and I don't want to be out of Jake's arms. I feel the helicopter land, but I still don't move.

"She asleep?" Someone asks.

"No," Jake softly answers, but he shifts his arms, sliding one under my knees.

Another set of hands remove the ear protection. I don't look to see who as Jake lifts me and carries me out.

My eyes are squeezed shut. I know I'm a mess when I hear the sound of another helicopter growing louder.

That makes my eyes snap open, panic lacing my voice. "Who's that?"

My arms clamp around Jake's neck as my entire body stiffens. "It's

Mason and Leo," he answers with a gentle squeeze. "They are here to help."

I shake my head. "Not help me," I whisper.

"Yes, help you," he answers and that's when I hear the steel in his voice. "They'll help or they'll answer to me."

I blink up at him, cocking my head. Jake is the oldest. The last of the original brothers. I suddenly wonder how much power he has in this dynamic.

My fingers spread out on his neck, twining in his hair. I must be an absolute mess, but he looks down at me, our eyes locking.

If I've never been weaker, he's never looked stronger.

His jaw is set in hard lines, his grey eyes flecked with steel.

Any tether I had to Toni is now gone. The bond with my family severed. I'm relieved.

But now is the time: I strike out on my own or I join this family for real. My lips softly part. "Jake?"

"Sweetheart."

"What happens if they don't? Help me..."

I feel his muscles tense under my body. "I promised what I promised, Nia, and I meant every word."

The other helicopter lands and Mason and Leo climb out. I'm at the point where I recognize a Kincaid, and the two brothers standing shoulder to shoulder exude the Kincaid confidence and swagger.

Roman and Luke join them, the four men shaking hands, giving one-armed hugs, before they all turn to look at me and Jake.

Jake hasn't moved, he has still has me in his arms, as the four men move toward us in a single line.

I live with a bunch of crazy criminals, and these four men might be the most intimidating thing I've ever seen.

They look like a wall, and I find myself shrinking a little deeper into Jake.

CHAPTER TWENTY-SEVEN

Jake

I put Nia in one of the bedrooms where she falls instantly asleep. I lay next to her for a few minutes just stroking her hair before I finally push up to find my family and my partners.

My current partners.

Because if they don't fall in line, we're going to have a brawl. That single punch I gave Toni wasn't even close to enough. If Nia hadn't been present, I might have kept going.

But she didn't need to see that. Or maybe she did.

But the state troopers certainly didn't. It's bad enough that I pulled a gun and punched him out. Not that there will be charges for either. Mason's lawyers are already working their magic.

We try to help them out by only dipping toes over the legal line, not large limbs.

But no one is going to arrest me if I clip Roman again. I saw the text that Nia read while I waited for her to wake up in the hospital. No wonder she bolted.

She knows they want to dump her and the way she's been clinging to me, she's worried they'll get their way.

Or maybe she's worried that I won't keep my word. Who could blame her? I told her we were there for a mutually beneficial relationship when I planned to set her free and let the Italians do their worst.

The very thought of it has my fists clenching as I step into the library at the back of the compound where the other Kincaids have already gathered.

They sit quietly, several of them holding drinks in their hands. Leo holds a beverage too, it's just Diet Coke. He gave up alcohol a few months ago.

"Jake," Roman says as he stands.

My finger points. "You really fucked up, Roman."

He holds up his hands. "The day did end with Toni in handcuffs."

"After Nia nearly died."

Leo clears his throat. I'm still getting used to him being delicate instead of charging into the conversation. "But she didn't. And we've accomplished our goal."

I don't like that answer at all. "How did you feel when Kim was in danger?"

Leo runs a hand through his hair. "First. Kim is pregnant. And my wife—"

I hold up my hand. "She was not your wife when little Anthony held a gun to her head."

"I know. And that's why we're here. Because Toni needed to be stopped."

"We're also here because you put out the call to protect Kim and we all answered," I remind him.

"What are you saying?" Mason sets his glass down and stands. "Are you putting out the call for us to protect Antonia?"

The room goes silent.

I feel my chest puff. Fuckers. "You aren't going to answer if I do?"

Mason shakes his head. "She's Toni's daughter," he starts. "She isn't like Charlotte and Kim."

I scrub my hands down my face. "You're right about that. She's much worse off than either of them."

Silence meets my words.

"Taking her into our family will cause far more problems than putting Toni in prison solves," Luke adds.

My mouth drops open as I look from man to man. I don't even know what to say to them. I knew they'd resist, but they haven't even asked a single question. They were all there when Toni tried to suffocate Nia with a pillow.

I turn around, stomping out of the library. "Where are you going?" Mason calls but I don't answer.

Opening the door to Nia's room, I stop, watching her sleep. "Baby girl?"

She doesn't move.

It's been shit day, I hate to wake her. So instead, I close the door behind me and walk over to the bed.

I was going to have her come plead her case, but I can't do it to her now. Afternoon sun tilts through the windows so I close the blinds and then slide into the bed next to her, place my hand on her hip.

I close my eyes too.

Those fuckers can wait.

CHAPTER TWENTY-EIGHT

NIA

I WAKE to find that it's dark outside. Jake is next to me in the bed, and I smile to see him. Somehow, him being here, next to me, is some confirmation that everything he said is true.

I stretch and push up. There is a bathroom attached to the bedroom, so I slip out of the bed, toss my clothes on the bathroom floor, and go to turn on the shower spray. Sliding open the glass door, I do a quick check.

Then I smile. That snake sure left an impression.

I let out the tiniest laugh because…well…I smiled. Today is un unlikely day to be happy, but all those tears have cleared out my soul.

And Jake stayed by my side all through the crying and after too.

I wash my hair and soap up my body, feeling a million times better as I turn the spray to cold and plunge my swollen face under.

Finally, feeling like myself, I step out and wrap up in a towel.

But that's when I notice, my clothes are gone.

"Jake?" I call out, my brow furrowed. "Did you take my clothes?"

"They were disgusting," he answers, poking his head into the bathroom with a half-smile. "Tomorrow, I'll get you more clothes but I thought for tonight, you could use my shirt and I could get your stuff clean."

"Your shirt?" I quirk a brow. "I suppose that will work. I can't walk around your family in nothing but a towel. It's weird enough…"

He pulls off his shirt, abs rippling as he pulls the white cotton over my head. It falls down to my mid thighs, completely covering my towel.

He tugs at the hem of the shirt and then reaches under, giving the towel one swift tug as it falls to the floor.

I let out a little gasp, mostly from surprise as a bit of heat fills my cheeks. "You didn't have to do that."

"Oh, I did. I like you in my shirt and only my shirt."

The warmth spreads down my neck. I like it too. It smells like him as it caresses my skin. "Just so long as no one sees me. This is not exactly how I want to greet your family."

"I don't care if they see you in my shirt," he murmurs, hooking a hand around my waist and pulling me close. "I want them to know you're mine."

My brows raise. "I don't think any of them are going to try and steal me away."

He dips his nose into my wet hair, rubbing the tip close to my ear. "They just need to understand what position you hold in this family."

"And what is that?"

"You're a queen, Nia."

I tip back to look at him, and he kisses my lips.

A knock sounds on the door. "Jake?"

"Yeah?" he calls back.

"We've got food. You both must be starving."

I haven't really been hungry, but his words spark my appetite. "Can we eat in here?"

"Why?"

A million reasons. "I'm not even wearing underwear."

He laughs and then lets me go and leaves the bathroom. I follow, watching him open the bedroom door just long enough to whisper to the person on the other side. A minute later Luke appears with a pair of basketball shorts in hand.

He gives me a small smile as he hands them to Jake. "For the lady."

I blink at them. "Are those shorts or capris?"

Both of them chuckle at that. All of these men are well over six feet and long shorts on me are practically going to be pants.

But I'd rather have my skin covered. Luke leaves again and I pull on the shorts, wrinkling my nose. "I don't think they're going to stay up."

"I'll roll the top."

"Or..." I give him my best smile. "We could just bring food back here."

He gives me a small smile. "I know it's been the longest day ever, but I really need them to hear some truths, and several can only be said by you."

I let out a deep sigh as I roll the shorts waistband one more time and then straighten my shoulders. "We really have to do this?"

He pulls me close. "We have all the fire power you'll ever need, sweetheart. I just need to make certain my family is on the same page."

I give a terse nod. He's right.

"I also want you to know, I've told them almost nothing that you shared with me about your cousins or your family. It's all information for you to dole out as you see fit."

My eyes go wide because it's never felt more like Jake is on my side. Fighting for me, even with his family.

And I do have a lot of valuable knowledge. As soon as my family finds out Toni is in prison, vying for his position will begin. And that means that I shouldn't delay either. With a sigh, I slip my hand into his and let him lead me down the hall.

But I nearly lose my nerve when we enter the kitchen and they're all standing around the island with drinks in hand.

Luke is the first to turn and greet us. "Hey, you two want a drink?"

"Bourbon," Jake answers.

"Shocking," Leo answers.

But I shake my head. "Just water."

"Water?"

"Nia's not much of a drinker," Jake says.

"And my head still hurts," I add with a deep breath, though that might have been a mistake. Reminding them of how I cracked up one of their cars, seems like a poor strategy.

"Water it is," Luke answers, opening up the fridge and pulling out a bottle of Evian.

I take it and the glass of ice, pouring myself a glass even as he hands me a wedge of lemon.

"Thank you," I say automatically, dropping the citrus into the beverage.

"You're welcome," Luke answers.

Mason is at the stove, stirring some rice dish, the smell of roasting meat coming from the oven. It smells amazing and my stomach rumbles.

"Have you eaten at all today?" Jake asks and I softly shake my head as several sets of dark eyes glance our way.

I squeeze his hand tighter.

"Get some sleep?" Mason asks his tone light and amicable.

"I did. Thank you."

A minute later, the meat comes out and plates are served, everyone settling around the massive island.

The food does wonders for my head and for my nerves as people push their plates back and I know the conversation I really don't want to have, but I'm far more prepared for, is about to start.

My hands are folded in my lap and as Mason clears his throat, Jake places his palm over both of mine. I unlace mine to grasp his and take a deep breath.

This isn't just about the Kincaids' support for me going forward. It's about what they need me to share, and this time, I understand my value.

But it's also about their original intentions, and that includes Jake. If they want me to share, they'll tell me the truth.

With my free hand, I fiddle with the basketball shorts skimming my knees.

"Nia," Mason says in his deep rumble that reverberates through me. "Why don't you start by telling us—"

My chin lifts and I look at the man who runs Kincaid operations. He is power and success, but I am forged from fire. I see it now. "Actually," my voice is only the smallest bit unsteady. "I think it's time that you all told me what you had planned for me."

"I don't—" Roman starts and my gaze shifts to his.

"Just so that we're clear, you people took me without permission. I could have told the police today. I didn't."

Silence meets my words.

My shoulders pull straighter. "The only person in this room, who has not broken several laws, is me."

More silence. I slide my hand out of Jake's. My feelings for him are real. But his are still a mystery to me, and this moment is about making sure the Kincaids do not chew me up and spit me out.

"Which means, we're going to start by you explaining why you have upended my entire life."

"Your father," Luke starts, and my gaze meets his, my defiance flashing in my eyes. "He deserved…" but Luke's voice tapers off.

"I am not just Toni's daughter," I answer quietly. "I am a person and however you justify what you did to me," and that's the moment I look at Jake, "it was wrong."

Jake's mouth pulls into a tight line. "You're right. It was."

"I've been a victim my whole life," I say to him. "I won't be yours."

He touches my shoulder, his fingers light. "They don't understand what you mean by that."

My brows draw together as I look back at Jake. "Don't understand what?"

"How you are a victim, sweetheart? I promised you I wouldn't share your secrets, and I didn't."

I swallow down a lump. It makes me feel so much better to know that he didn't tell them what I'd shared in confidence. "Did you tell me the truth about your father?"

"Every word," he answers back, with a wince.

I nod, some of my bravado whooshing out of me. His fingers slide down my arm, reaching for my hand, and pulling me lightly from the chair. "May I please share some of the things you told me?"

Shame pierces my gut. "I want to know first, what your intentions were. You never planned to help me, did you?"

I don't know why, but I need to hear him say it. That Roman's text this morning was true, and he always planned to dump me. That the ring still on my finger is a lie.

"Before I met you," he answers with a grimace, "I intended to use you as a way to get information on Toni."

I pull my hand from his. I appreciate the truth, but it hurts even more than I thought it would.

But he reaches for my fingers again. "But that plan changed very quickly, Nia. You have to know that."

I shake my head. "I'm not sure..."

He moves close enough that I can feel his heat. "I'm going to say this to you, in front of them. I've done my duty to my family. Fulfilled my promises to them. The rest of the promises are yours, sweetheart."

My throat closes as I swallow several times. "You mean that?"

"Every word I've said." He touches my face, and I can't believe it, but there are some tears left in my eyes. "We are forged..."

"...in the fire," I reply with a shaky breath. "Jake..."

"Yeah, baby girl?"

"I think I might love you," I whisper as his forehead comes to meet mine.

"I love you too," he answers, kissing me in front of his whole family. I breathe him in, closing my eyes.

"Where does that leave us?" I hate the question, or maybe I'm just worried I'll hate the answers.

His arms come around me, gently pulling me close. "I'll tell you whatever you need to know about us. But we need you to do some sharing too. It's time for truth and for a new plan."

CHAPTER TWENTY-NINE

JAKE

I CAN SEE by her face that's she's angry. It's in the defiant tilt of her chin. "Is that what you and your family need? For me to share?"

I might have chosen my words poorly there. What I really want is for her to help me convince them to help us. But I'm threading a needle here.

I don't want either party to think I've switched sides. I want everyone to understand that we are all on the same side.

And that everyone here can help each other.

But I'm also a hundred percent certain, if my family won't help Nia, she and I are gone. So maybe I am switching sides. I'll always love my nephews, but I won't abandon Nia. She is my future.

Which is why, I'd like to be delicate here.

But fuck me, like I've said, I'm an old-school gangster and subtle negotiation is not my strength.

It's Mason's.

I look at my oldest nephew, the lynch pin in our new business, and I hold his gaze.

His brothers and Luke, they all show him deference. Not me. I am their uncle, the patriarch of this family.

I allow him to lead us in business because he's the most apt.

But I am this family's boss, and perhaps it's time that I made that clear. But that doesn't mean I shouldn't offer a few carrots.

"I need them to understand that you, Nia, have the answers and a vested interest in sharing the truth with them."

Her eyes go from defiant to confused, as I gently turn her around and start pulling the hem of my shirt up her legs and around her waist.

Her hands stop me, her gaze meeting mine, now shining with fear.

"Just your torso, love," I whisper close to her ear.

"You know how much I hate for people to see that," she replies, her voice trembling with emotion.

"You're a warrior, Nia. All warriors carry battle wounds."

I hear a few men suck in their breath, but I don't look at them. Nia's spine straightens again, her face hardening in resolute lines as she gives a nod of agreement.

Gently, slowly, I lift the shirt, revealing her lower back and ribs.

"Christ," Mason rumbles as Leo makes a feral sound in his throat.

Holding the shirt in one hand, I turn her so they see the front, both the marks on her body and the hurt in her eyes. They will not ignore her pain as they make decisions.

"You can drop the shirt, Jake," Roman says, his tone clipped as he turns his head to the side.

But it's Nia's hand that takes the shirt from mine and leaves the fabric gathered under her breasts. "Roman."

He looks back at her, as he draws in a long breath through his nose.

Luke shifts. "Who gave those to you?"

"Toni," she answers quietly.

"But only you? Not Jess?" Mason asks as he assesses her.

Nia looks at me and I give her a nod to continue. "Only me," she confirms. "And only when he suffers some major loss."

"So every time we've hit him," Leo's fists are clenched as he crosses his arms over his massive chest, "he hits you."

She shrugs. "That's about right."

"But not Jess?" Roman repeats.

I had half forgotten that Jess was under the protection of the family. I look at Nia, asking permission, and she gives a small nod. "Nia isn't his biological daughter. Maria had an affair."

"Wait—" Leo rumbles. "Do not tell me—"

"Nia's twenty. She's not your long-lost sister," I answer back, quickly shutting that down. "But she has little loyalty to Toni and a great deal of knowledge of the inner workings of the family."

"And the business," Nia adds with a shrug. "When you don't talk much, you hear a lot."

Roman leans down on the counter, resting on his elbows. "So you think you can help us...what?"

But Leo holds up a hand. "It's not that I don't appreciate what you've been through, but try to understand, in protecting you, we put the rest of us in danger. And it's not just us as men, our women, my child."

"You put yourself in danger when you took me. Don't put that on me," she says raising up her chin. "What I am offering are real solutions to minimize the damage, which you created," she points a finger. "And like every negotiation, I'm hoping to get something out of this too. This family's protection."

"And if we say no?" Mason asks.

I step closer to Nia, wrapping my arm around her. I love my family, my nephews, but I've been a soldier for them, for their women. "I promised you that I would put Toni in prison. I fulfilled that promise. In addition, I have stood by your side, Mason, and yours, Leo, to help you keep your women safe. If you turn Nia out today, I go with her."

"Jake," Luke bites out. "What the fuck?"

"Nia and I are getting married," my hands spread out on her back as I speak. "She will be my first priority. If you are not going to give back to me what I have given to you, then we are done."

I slash my gaze over them.

It's Roman who speaks first. "I'm in for helping Nia." Then he looks at Nia. "I am sorry for the text and the damage it caused."

She gives the smallest jerk of her chin in acknowledgment.

"I'm in too," Luke adds. "But I think Mason and Leo should return to their wives once we're done here and let the single men handle this one."

A collective murmur of agreement rumbles through the group.

Over the next half hour, Nia explains which casinos make the most profit, which should be sold, which cousins have the most even tempers and the best minds for business. "You want the three Andriani brothers. They aren't like the others. Smart and level-headed, they'll take a deal that leaves them with a few of the more profitable casinos and gets rid of some dead weight."

By the time she's done, Mason is smiling in the way he only does when he knows he's going to win. "This is good," he murmurs. "And Nia…"

"Yes?"

"Welcome to the family."

Nia blushes, her hand finding mine. I give her the smallest tug, because it's time for my woman and me to go to bed.

CHAPTER THIRTY

NIA

I LOOK BACK as Jake and I walk away, every set of Kincaid eyes staring back at me. It makes my face heat all over again.

The last half hour was…intense.

But the plan is solid. And by some miracle, I trust Jake to keep his promises. I can't believe that could be true.

Here I am, though. If I'm wrong…well, I'm wrong. But at least I tried. Really tried living and not just hiding. And I don't just mean from Toni.

Making choices based on fear is a different sort of fear-based living, and I've participated in that wholeheartedly.

"Can I ask you a question?" I say as we turn the corner and start up the stairs.

"Anything."

"What is your role at Kincaid Enterprises?"

"Security," he answers with a wink.

"Oh. That is helpful," I grip his fingers tighter as I move closer, pressing closer to his side.

"You know what Mason does. Roman runs the casinos, Leo the nightclubs, and Luke is in charge of the construction of the underground tunnel that will connect our various casinos with those of the families that partner with us. It's that project that began your father's demise because Mason intentionally left the Diamond out of the plans, devaluing the property."

I'd heard scraps of this in the house.

"Luke is in charge of that project? I had assumed it was Mason."

"His plan, he got all the permitting. But the actual building of the tunnel goes to Luke. He got a degree in engineering and everything."

My eyes widen in surprise. They really aren't the typical gangsters Vegas is filled with otherwise.

"And Mason?"

"Yeah. All the schooling at only the best," Jake says, as he slides my hand from his left to his right so that he can put his arm around me. "Dartmouth. Harvard Law School."

"And you?"

He shakes his head, but I see the grimace. "Old-school gangster, remember?"

"But how did you learn all the modern technology then?"

He squeezes my hip. "It's interesting so I studied it all myself. If I had it to do over, I'd get a formal degree, though. I'd develop technologies instead of just using them."

I cock my head. "Why not do it now?"

He raises his brows. "My share in Kincaid is worth over a billion dollars."

I nearly trip. "Wait. A billion?"

He stops in the hall. "Yeah, sweetheart. A billion. I was going to sell my shares. Open my own company. But with you joining us, I think I'll stay."

"Jake…"

He gives me a soft smile. "Don't think I'm giving something up. I've actually gained all the perspective I needed."

"You're sure?"

"Very. Which means whatever dreams you have after this is all over, are yours for the taking."

My mouth opens and closes. I lick my suddenly dry lips. "So, if I wanted to try my hand at singing?"

"I'll have Leo book you in our clubs. I'd say that you'd need to audition, but I've heard you. You'll bring the crowds for sure."

I blink at him. "Jake?"

"Yeah?"

"I think having a billion dollars means you get to do whatever you want. If you want to study, develop technology, you should. Mason's a smart guy, I bet you could sell him on the fact that it would be to his advantage."

His chin draws back as he stares down at me. "So you, at twenty, are going to work, and me, at thirty-five, is going to go to school?"

This might be the most normal and best conversation of my life. It's so wonderful that a giggle escapes my lips. Making plans, sharing dreams...

This is what I've been waiting for. This is where I wanted to go when I ran. "I could go to school too. I could get like a performing arts degree or something."

His brows shoot up. "Can we study together? There are all sorts of little nooks and crannies in the library."

Another laugh falls from my lips. "You are so bad, Daddy."

He rumbles out his appreciation a moment before his hands grab my ass, and he lifts me in his arms, carrying me the rest of the way down the hall.

I give a squeal, my arms wrapping about his neck when I hear one of the men, Leo I think, yell up the stairs. "Jake, don't even tell me your as loud as Mason. It's bad enough—"

"Get ear plugs, you big fucking baby!" Jake yells back before his mouth captures mine.

The kiss isn't sweet, our mouths devour as our tongues tangle. I thread my fingers into his hair.

I don't even notice we've stepped into the room until he kicks the door closed, the resounding thud makes me pull back an inch or two to look down in his face. "I can be quiet. I think."

"Fuck that."

"It is strange not being alone. There were no people for miles when we were at the little house," I say with a wistful sigh, before he threads one of his hands into my hair, pulling my mouth back down to his.

"You pretend we're there, baby girl," he answers when our lips finally unlock. "And we can go for as long as you want for our honeymoon."

"You really want to get married?" I ask, nipping at my lip. "We don't have to."

"We're a lot alike. We both wanted to go it alone, didn't we?"

I nod. It's so true.

"I say we both commit to being in this together. All the way, for the rest of our lives."

Did I just suggest quiet? My legs wrap around his waist, my mouth dropping back to his.

His cock is grinding into me as I roll my hips. He squeezes my ass, pulling me even closer.

We're still standing in the middle of the room, my hands sliding up and down the bare skin of his back. Part of me wants to climb off him if only to strip down and feel more of his skin.

But part me doesn't want to move. This might be the most perfect embrace, and I'm not sure I want it to end.

A knock at the door makes the decision for me.

Jake growls into my mouth before he breaks the kiss. Still holding, he barks out. "What?"

"Nia's clothes are done," Roman calls. "Luke and I are going to the cabin to collect more of your things."

Jake sets me down, finally, and crosses the room, opening the door just enough to talk with Roman. "You interrupted me for laundry?"

Roman chuckles. "And to tell you that Mason and Leo are leaving. You'll have the house to yourself."

I slide over to the bed, kicking off the ridiculous shorts so that I'm in nothing but his T-shirt, as I lay down, propping up on my elbows, legs exposed, hair tumbling over one shoulder.

A moment later, he closes the door and turns back, stopping as he looks at me.

I slide one foot up my other calf. "We're going to be alone?"

"That's right, baby girl," he says in a growl, pulling at the button on his jeans. "Why don't you be a good girl and take off that shirt?"

I push up onto my knees, spreading them apart as I grab the hem and dance it up to my waist. "And if I want to be a bad girl?"

He yanks his pants down his hips, his cock springing out, already leaking a bit of precum.

My tongue darts out to lick my lips. "Shirt," he growls as he stalks toward me, the movement of his muscles holding me transfixed for a moment.

He reaches me and grabs the shirt himself, pulling it over my head, as my arms raise too.

The moment it's over my head, I pitch forward, flicking my tongue out to lick the pearl of liquid.

He makes a feral noise in the back of his throat as he threads his hand back into my hair, pulling me down.

My lips part, allowing his cock to sink into my mouth and slide against my tongue. "Fuck me," he rumbles as I sink all the way down, holding him in my mouth as he hits the back of my throat.

I choke a bit, but I don't let up. I like holding him in my mouth like this. The little bit of sacrifice only making me feel closer to him.

I look at up at him, his grey eyes so intense, that I can't look away as I slowly pull back, his cock now slick with my saliva.

"Jesus, Nia. You're killing me."

"How's that, Daddy?"

"I love you so much, sweetheart."

I blink the bit of water from my eyes. "I love you too."

"Which is why, I'm going to fuck you six ways to Sunday, tonight."

I look up at him for a minute, before I fall back onto the bed, my arms going over my head. "Fuck me, Daddy."

CHAPTER THIRTY-ONE

JAKE

MY FINGERS SKIM over the arch of her foot, circling her ankle, before I slide them over the inside of her calf along her knee and up her thigh. Her legs fall open for me and another satisfied growl fills my chest.

I'm going to lose myself in Nia and I can't wait.

I don't just mean the sex.

She's rewriting every part of my life, filling the white spaces between the black lines with color.

My thumb parts her sex and glides over her folds, her body arching into me. Part of me wants to climb on top of her and do exactly what I said.

Fuck her six ways to Sunday.

But even more than that, I might want to make love to her. Which is why my thumb makes a second gentle pass, her hips rolling with my stroke.

She's already slick with excitement as I sink into her, filling her tight pussy with my single digit.

Her back arches, her fingers twining into the sheets. "More."

I smile, but even I know it's wolfish. "Patience."

I take my thumb back out, teasing her clit as I watch her skin flush, her nipples tighten. I think I could do this all night.

"Jake," she moans, her head thrashing, twisting up her halo of blonde hair.

In answer to her plea, I use my other hand to hook her knee, opening her legs wider to accommodate my shoulders as I sink my upper half on the bed.

And then I trace the exact same path with my tongue.

She starts to pant, her body moving with me, her hands clenching and unclenching in the sheets. Her scent fills my nostrils, her taste in my mouth, and I swear, I just want to devour her.

I slide a finger inside her as she clenches around me. I want to tease her, draw this out, but I'm as desperate for her orgasm as I am for my own.

I need to feel her. To connect. To make her mine.

Her thighs begin to tremble around my head, and I slide a second finger inside her, curling them just so to stroke that place that I know will send her over the edge.

She gasps out a breathy moan as her thighs clamp around my head. "Jake."

I swirl my tongue around her clit increasing the pressure as she lets out a keening moan.

Her pussy is gripping my fingers like a vise while her back arches in the sexiest fucking way. It drives me crazy.

She finally breaks, her cries filling the room. But I hardly let her come down before I'm climbing up her body and sliding inside her.

I want her in the worst way.

I slip inside her slowly, making sure she's ready for me. If there is one thing I'm not interested in, it's hurting my girl.

She stretches around me, her tight pussy wet enough that I manage to push in until I'm balls deep.

I groan it feels so good as her fingers grip my waist, holding me inside her body. It's this moment of deep connection she likes to draw out, and I like it too.

"You feel so good, baby."

"So do you," she moans her heels digging into the backs of my upper legs. "I could stay like this forever."

"Took the words right out of my mouth." But that's the moment that I start to pull out. Because as good as this feels, I know I can do better.

And I'm done talking. I want to show Nia how much I need her. And so, I lean down, kissing her with lips, tongue, and teeth as I pump in and out of her.

It doesn't take long for the pace to rachet up, my thrusts matching her breathy cries as she goes from panting to moaning, her heels now digging into my ass as she works me to go harder, faster.

My fingers twine with hers, lifting them over her head as I go harder. Her face is red as she breaks from the kiss to let out a keening cry.

I can feel her pussy clamping around me, her body so close she's going to break.

Which is why, I slow down…

She digs a heel in deep, giving me what some might consider a kick. "Don't stop."

I chuckle, liking a girl who is willing to get a little rough. But also, I'm not a man who gets bossed.

So instead, I roll, lifting her a bit as I flip us around so that I'm on my back with Nia on top of me. "You want to drive, do you, sweetheart?"

I've got to be honest, I can't wait to see Nia on top. I'm not disappointed. She pushes up on my chest, her arms squeezing her tits together, her hips flared as her thighs hug mine.

It's so hot, I groan as I grab her hips in my hands and push her tighter into my body. I know her clit grinds into my pelvic bone when her eyes roll back. "Holy shit."

Lifting her the smallest bit, I slide her back down, pressing her hard into me again. Her heads lulls back, her body arching and pushing her chest out even more. Fuck me, my cock is leaking as I hold back.

We're cumming at the same time, which means my little man is going to have to deal.

She lifts up on her own, and then slides back down me, setting a pace that has her jiggling in all the right places.

My teeth grind as I start spitting words of encouragement. I have never wanted to cum more than I do in this moment, but delaying is this form of perfect torture as her fingers curl into chest hair, her back so bowed, I know she's close. "You tell me, baby. Tell me when you're going to cum."

I'm pulling us tight together on the down thrusts, feeling her thighs tremble around me. "I'm close. So close…"

"That's it, baby." I'm pushing up into her, feeling the vibrations of her body. It's so good, my teeth clench. I want to squeeze my eyes shut, but I don't want to miss the sight of her when she breaks apart.

"Jake…" she gasps. "Oh God, Jake, I'm going to…."

That's all I need to hear. With a roar, I start shooting cum inside her even as she spasms around me, letting out a loud moan.

It goes on and on, the orgasm both intense and so long, I think it might never end.

But finally, Nia collapses on my chest. "Wow."

"Yeah."

Her cheek burrows into my chest, her body limp against mine. "That was…"

"The best," I answer for her. Because we're at the finish-each-other's-sentences stage.

She lifts her cheek and smiles at me, soft and a little dreamy. "Glad you think so too. I don't have anything to compare it too."

I squeeze her tightly, kissing the top of her head. "It's special, Nia. Like everything between us."

She snuggles deeper. "That's good."

I'm still inside her, our bodies twined together. She's so soft, I wonder if she's asleep when she lifts her head. "How is doggie?"

"What?"

"Well, you said we couldn't do doggie for my first time. How would it be now?"

Fuck me, but my cock starts growing inside her. "If you're not careful, baby girl, you'll wake the beast. And considering how new you are at this, we ought to give you a little rest."

She nips at her lip. "Good point. We'll wait until tomorrow."

I don't tell her, it's already tomorrow. I might be old, but I'm not that old.

But she lays her head back down and this time, I feel her drift off, her body twitching as she falls to sleep.

Sliding her to the side, I wrap my arm around her back, keeping her close so she's cradled against my body. Warm. Safe.

It's been a long day, and my girl needs some sleep.

CHAPTER THIRTY-TWO

NIA

I WAKE with the first rays of the sun, Jake's hand stroking down my spine. "Did you sleep?" I ask, lifting my sleepy gaze to his.

"Enough," he murmurs and then drops a kiss into my hair.

"Enough?" I ask, pushing even further up to meet his gaze again. "How long is that? How long have you been awake?"

"An hour?"

"What have you been doing?"

"Watching you sleep," he gives me that half grin that always makes me crazy hectic inside.

But it's the words that really twist up my insides. "Watching me sleep? Why?"

"You're so beautiful, Nia," he answers, lifting his hand to skim his fingers down my cheek. "I can't believe you're mine."

"Yours," I say with a smile. "Maybe you're mine."

"Oh, I am," he rolls us both until he's on top of me. "I told you. I am your soldier, sweetheart."

I wrap my hands around his neck, our mouths crashing together as our legs tangle. I love this part. All right, fine, I love all the parts when it comes to Jake. But this intimacy of skin against skin, of the way the hair on his chest feels, the rough skin of his hands...

It's intoxicating. And before I know it, my breath is coming out in jagged little bursts.

My legs have come around his waist and his cock is pressing into me. I roll my hips, allowing him to sink in a little deeper as we both groan.

But he pulls back out. I give a small cry of protest.

He only laughs. "Don't worry, baby girl, I'm going to give you what you want. But I think you might be ready to try something new?"

Excitement pulses through me. "What kind of new?"

But before he answers, he flips me onto my belly, settling between my legs.

I open for him, so ready for whatever he's got in mind. Jake grabs my hips, lifting my ass up as he sinks inside me.

It's more of everything in this position and my eyes go wide as I look back over my shoulder at him.

One of his hands braces on the bed, as the other slides over my stomach and then between my legs, his middle finger pressing into my clit.

I buck against him, making his cock slide out an inch before he pushes back in. "You like that?"

"Yeah, Daddy." My eyes close as he slowly starts to circle my clit before he pulls out, pushing back in at the same slow pace that drives me crazy.

The pleasure builds, my body his to tease and stroke.

His mouth comes to my neck, his lips, tongue and teeth nipping and sucking at my skin as he slowly picks up the pace.

My hands twist into the sheets, my ass in the air as my back arches so far back, I'm bent near in half.

Faster and higher we climb, the slap of our bodies only covered by the moans that I can't keep in.

Everything we do is better than the last, and I hear myself start to beg. "More," I gasp out. "Harder."

He makes a snarling, guttural groan as he pumps into me, my body so taut, I think I might break.

And then I do, screaming out my finish as I orgasm, my pussy gripping his cock like a vise.

Three more thrusts and he cums too, his roar echoing through the room.

I collapse onto the bed, sure that I won't be able to move for a week.

So why do I ask the question, "What else have we not done?"

His forehead is pressed to my back, and I feel him shake his head. "Woman. You're going to kill me."

I reach back and give his ass a light slap. "Keep up."

He snorts a laugh, but I feel his cock growing inside me again. Shit.

But instead of thrusting his hips, he pulls back, lifting me in his arms.

"Where are we going?"

"Shower," he answers. "We can discuss how I'm keeping up with you pressed against the shower wall."

"Oh," I gasp, my own body heating up.

It takes us close to an hour before we're finally done in the shower.

By the time we've finished, I'm famished, but too satiated to move quickly.

Jake dries me off and then wraps me in a towel. "Luke and Roman went to get your clothes. I'm just going to find them and then we'll get some breakfast."

"Mmm," I hum, his hands still on my body. He kisses my lips as he slings a towel around his hips and disappears from the bathroom. I follow, leaving the bathroom in time to see him open the bedroom door, two suitcases just outside.

"His and hers," he says with a grin as he pulls first one and then the other into the bedroom.

My eyes widen. "Did your nephews pack my underwear?"

"Probably Roman," Jake mutters, his smile disappearing. "Fucker is hellishly good with the details and usually very good at attending a lady's needs."

"So it's just me he doesn't like?" That hurts. I've been part of a family that didn't want me before. There is a part of me that thinks Roman doesn't like me because...I'm not likable.

"It's Toni he doesn't like. Trust me, if he packed your stuff and agreed to help you, he's on your side, Nia."

I don't argue as I open the larger case and find my clothes. Pulling out some jeans and a T-shirt, I quickly dress.

Sighing, I run a brush through my hair, letting it cascade down my shoulders. I'm so thrilled to be part of Jake's life. But I wonder if these insecurities will ever disappear. I'm not just marrying a man but his family too.

I have this urge to speak with my sister. She'd know just how to handle all of this. "Jake?"

"Yeah, baby girl?"

"Can I talk to Jess?"

He gives me a soft smile. "Absolutely. Let's get you breakfast and then Roman can make the call for you."

Roman. Great.

CHAPTER THIRTY-THREE

NIA

JESS'S VOICE calms some of the hectic inside me. "And then Daddy went completely crazy and locked me in my room and told me that I was marrying this old man from Italy," she says in a rush. "And that's when Mike broke down my door and got me out of there."

I keep listening as minutes tick by. Jess details all that's happened to her since I left that night for my date with Gris. And though I had questions, somehow just hearing her voice has soothed some of the worry. "I'm so glad he was able to get you out."

"Me too. Now tell me what happened to you. Mike says you're not with Gris but with a Kincaid?"

I wince, not having thought this part through. "It's a really long story," I say breezily. "But Jake's amazing and he asked me to marry him."

"Oh my God, that is the best!" I'm glad my sister isn't asking the details. "Mike," she shrieks, "Jake and Nia are getting married."

"Jake?" I hear a male rumble in the background. "Holy shit."

I let out a long breath. "It's a little complicated though because I don't think Roman likes me."

"Cause you're Toni's kid?" she asks, as though it's completely obvious. Maybe it is.

"I think so."

Jess hums like she understands. "Give it time, Nia. You're really hard not to like."

That might be the nicest thing she's ever said to me, and I melt into the kitchen chair. The guys all nicely cleared out, retreating to their rooms after Roman handed me his phone.

He called Mike so that it looks like a call between cousins, just in case anyone is checking.

"You really think so?" I bite my lip, fiddling with the hem of my shirt before drawing my knees up. "Because I'm not sure I can be in another family where I'm the outsider, you know?"

"Who says you were the outsider? Toni was the outsider. Me, the aunts, the Andrianis, we have always been your family, not his. The only people he got were the Vendettis and that's because they are psychos."

I smile despite myself. "You mean that?"

"I mean it," she answers softly. "Now, give me a few tips on getting Mike to propose."

"You don't want a bigger fish?" I whisper darting my eyes to make sure no one is listening.

"No," Jess says back, quiet too. "I'm good with the fish who breaks down the door and literally carries me to safety."

I nip at my lip. "Well, your blowjobs have gotten you this far."

She laughs. "Word."

A small silence settles between us. "I wish I could hug you."

"Me too. I wish I could see you or at least tell you where I am, but Mike told me not to say on the phone."

"I totally understand, I know we're leaving today, but I don't even know where."

Jess sighs. "Think we'll get to see each other soon?"

"I hope so," I answer. "I miss you."

"I miss you too."

"I love you, Jess. Thanks for always being there."

"I love you too. And ditto. I can't wait to get to live a real life together, instead of that lie."

I did not give my sister enough credit. "Me too. Take care, okay?"

"I will. You too."

I nod, then I realize she can't see me. "I will. Talk soon."

We hang up and I sit there for a while, staring at Roman's phone. My head is full, I guess.

"Done?" Jake calls from the doorway. I have no idea how much time has passed, but I was totally lost in thought. "Yes. Tell Roman thank you for helping me make the call."

"You can tell him yourself," Jake replies as he turns back toward the stairs. "We're ready!"

Roman and Luke appear thirty seconds later with our suitcases in hand.

I push up from the chair giving Roman his phone back. "Thanks for that."

"You're welcome," he answers, not meeting my eyes.

I nip at my lip, knowing that I misjudged my sister the way Roman did me. "I get why you don't like me."

His gaze snaps to mine. "I like you a lot, Nia."

My brow furrows. "What?"

"The mistake was mine, and it was a matter of not knowing you," he says with a shrug. "I'm sorry for what I texted, for what I started. It won't happen again."

I nod. I get it.

I reach for my suitcase, but he gives me a wink. "I got it."

We leave the house, a large SUV waiting in the drive. Piling in, it only takes five minutes before we've reached a small air strip.

The plane that waits on the runway is small, but it looks ridiculously nice. My family has money, but not private-jet money.

I stop, my brows going up, as my sunglasses come down. "We're flying in that?"

"Private planes and private air strips make it far easier to doctor flight logs," Jake murmurs, his arm coming around me.

"Do I get to know where we're going?"

"Marathon, Florida," he says. "If we're going to hide, it might as well be on a beach."

My lips part. "Seriously?"

"Like I said, private airstrip."

"We'll probably stay for four or five days and then move locations. But we'll try to keep our stops scenic."

I can't even imagine the money they're spending to fly private planes about every four or five days.

"Jake says you have a passport?" Roman asks, pulling out his phone like he's making a note or something.

I nod. Using it would mean alerting customs of our movements.

The car stops and Jake gets out, holding out his hand so that I slide across the seat on his side.

"I'll work on getting you another…" Roman says as he gets out too but stops halfway when his phone starts buzzing. He glances down. "It's Mason."

"Better pick it up," Jake answers, pulling me tighter into his side.

"Mason?" Roman starts but instantly stops, his face going granite hard.

"What's wrong?" Luke asks but Roman doesn't have time to answer. Because another black SUV is racing toward us.

"Shit," Jake rumbles, tossing his suitcase to the side and tucking me partially behind him.

"What's happening?" I cry.

Roman holds a hand out in front of me, further blocking me from view. "Toni has escaped."

CHAPTER THIRTY-FOUR

JAKE

I DON'T NEED any more information to know he is barreling toward us at eighty miles an hour.

It's fucking Toni.

And that fucker is going down. "Get Nia in the car," I snarl at Roman, who responds instantly by wrapping an arm around her and tucking her into his body.

One of the doors on Toni's SUV flies open and a goon with a gun hangs out as several shots ring out on the airfield. I recognize Gio Vendetti as we all duck, Roman covering Nia with his larger frame.

I say a quick and silent thank you to my nephew as I pull my Glock from my waistband, popping off a shot.

Not at Gio, but at the gas tank. I'll deal with that piece of shit later.

The ping of the hit echoes through the open air and we all know that the car is about to blow.

The pilot must see it too because the plane revs up, beginning to taxi down the runway to the far end.

Which is a good call, we don't need to add jet fuel to the inferno that's about to ignite.

All the doors to the SUV open, five men jump out of the car.

I only care about one.

I set my sights on Toni, even as more bullets begin to pepper the air.

Luke has his pistol out too and he returns fire.

I level my gun, aiming right for Toni's chest.

He raises his hands as his men cease fire. Standing between them, he glares at me. "I want my daughter. That's all."

"The one you tried to suffocate with a pillow?" I bark back. "I don't think so."

"I'm doing you a favor, Jake," Toni calls. "She'll never be faithful to you."

"You're confusing her with yourself," I growl back. I don't believe it for a second. I was there when Nia chose me over escape. I know her wounds like I know my own.

The ones this fucker gave her.

If I give her love, the kind that isn't selfish, she'll be mine forever.

"She isn't yours," Toni snarls. "Hand her over and I'll end the vendetta between us. I'll surrender another casino, you'll get your tunnel."

I shake my head. "We're getting your casino and our tunnel either way, old man."

He shakes his head. "That's what you think."

I have no idea what he's got planned and I don't care. I'll surrender Nia over my dead body. "No. That's what you think. Admit it, Toni. You've lost."

He snarls and quick as a snake, he raises his gun. Mine comes up too, both firing at the same moment.

I barely feel the prick in my arm as my shot hits him square in the chest.

One of the other men pops off another shot at Luke before they all scatter.

Luke volleys several more shots, but I don't think he hits anyone as they keep running.

"You go," Luke cries over the noise of the plane. "Get out of here before the car blows."

"But—" This is a big mess to clean up.

The plane stops again, further down the runway. Luke might be right. If we don't get out of here, we might never leave. Then again, as the man in charge of security, I have the most justifiable reason for shooting. Toni fired first.

It's Roman who is still holding Nia tight. "We got it, big guy. Go. Get her out of here."

"But I'm the one with the license to..."

"We're not going through police," Roman murmurs. "He's a wanted man and he's going to disappear like one." He places a hand on my shoulder. "Now, you get out of here and get yourself patched up."

"Patched up?"

That's when I look down to see my arm covered with blood. "Fuck."

"He shot you," Nia says on a gasping breath. "You're hurt."

Maybe it's the adrenaline but I barely feel a thing. "I'll be fine, sweetheart."

She's pushes out of Roman's grip, falling toward me, and wraps her arms around my waist. "Let me see it."

"On the plane, love. You can check on the plane. But we've got to go."

She gives a shaky nod as I wrap my other arm around her, and we climb back into our car.

Nia slides over the bench seat as I get in next to her. She instantly starts fussing with my shirt, assessing the blood. "Do you think it hit the bone? Can you move the arm? Did the bullet exit?"

Roman climbs into the passenger seat and Luke is already in the driver's seat. The moment the doors are closed, he speeds off toward the plane.

"Nia, I promise, I'll be fine. We should be talking about you. Toni is dead."

Roman and Luke exchange glances as I watch the woman I love. I just shot her father…

She shakes her head. "Toni was dead to me a long time ago." She squeezes me tighter. "You're my family, which is why, the second that door closes, you're showing me the wound."

Roman meets my gaze over the top of Nia's head. I know that he is realizing the depths to which he had it wrong. But Nia turns to him. "We'll need a doctor."

"I'll take care of it, Nia," he answers in a reassuring voice as we reach the plane.

It's then that Toni's car blows. Our car rocks with the blast and despite my arm, I hug Nia close, shielding her.

"Don't worry," Luke says pointing at the windshield. "Bulletproof glass."

My arm is starting to ache, and I'll be glad to be settled into one of the seats of the plane with some bourbon in hand, Nia tucked into my side as we fly far away from here.

Roman opens the door. "I'm going to speak to the pilot, see if he can take off with Toni's car still on the runway."

I grimace, realizing we have a witness outside the family. "Who's the pilot?"

"Don't worry," Luke catches my gaze. "It's a friend."

I'm not sure what he's getting at. I'm normally better at reading the meaning of his words but my arm is really starting to ache now and my head hurts.

Roman and Luke retrieve the bags from the back of the car and carry them up the stairs, behind us.

We enter the low-lit interior of the plane, and I immediately sit in one of the large leather captain's chairs, my eyes closing.

I let out a long breath. My arm hurts like hell, but I can also feel that it's a fleshy muscle wound and not the bone.

A few stitches, some antibiotics, and I'll be good as new.

That doesn't stop Nia from starting to fuss.

She starts undoing the buttons of my shirt, pulling it off my body. "I'm fine, sweetheart," I murmur but she only clucks her tongue.

"You'll let me be the judge of that."

"Ever treat a bullet wound?" A slick accented voice calls from the front of the plane.

Nia lets go of my shirt, spinning.

My eyes widen as I try to glance around the amazing curve of her ass. Is that Gris?

If it is, that man is about to be toast.

CHAPTER THIRTY-FIVE

Nia

I'm going to kill that Brit with my bare hands.

In this moment, I've never felt more like a phoenix rising.

"From the ashes," I murmur, and I know Jake hears me by the way he shifts in his seat.

I take two steps toward the man coming out of the cockpit, my teeth gnashing together when I realize something is wrong.

Even in the shadow of the doorway, I can see that he doesn't look quite right. The nose, the eyes, the cut of his hair.

"Nia," Luke clears his throat. "Meet Triston Smith."

My chin pulls back. "Triston?"

The Brit shrugs. "Our mother pulled most of our names from the family tree. I think I fared far better than my brother, Griswold." And then he gives me a wicked grin.

Luke starts for the door. "I'm going to patrol the perimeter, make sure none of our friends circle back."

I don't turn away from Triston. He knows exactly who I thought he was. "How is your brother?" I ask, intentionally making my voice sugary-sweet.

I know that I only just gained the trust of the Kincaids and I don't have a lot of room here, but then again, my cousins are a lynch pin in this plan and I'm no wilting flower.

"He's good. Yourself?"

"Very well," I say, waving my hand with the ring.

Behind me, Jake chuckles. "This is going to be fun."

I look back at him and he gives me a wink. It tells me that I have his support for whatever I say next. Which is good. Because Gris and I have a debt to settle.

I see Triston's slight wince and I know that he knows....

"That's wonderful that he's doing so well," I say, my chin rising. "Because the rest of us have been through hell."

Triston takes a step forward. "Now listen, it seems to me you ended up with a pretty good deal so—"

"Big mistake," Jake mutters behind me, but Triston hears him and stops.

"Will the police be coming, do you think?" This is a question I ask Roman, not Triston.

"No," Roman shakes his head. "There is no one around here to report anything."

"Then the cleanup can wait for Gris to arrive?" I say with a smile. "Someone is going to have to bury my father's body." I put emphasis on the last word because this has been anything but a good deal.

I know I'm moving toward a good place. I'm supposed to be with Jake. But that doesn't change all the fear I endured, or the fact that I had to have the kind of standoff with Toni that is the stuff of nightmares.

Jake...he's paid for his part. He's bleeding in a chair because he took on my fight. It was me Toni wanted dead, and it was Jake who saved me.

But Gris will pay for what he did just like the rest of us. Make no mistake. My spine stiffens along with my resolve. Am I hurt and angry about everything that went down today? Maybe.

Does Gris get to just walk away a winner? Definitely not.

Triston brushes past me and kneels in front of Jake. "Let me look."

Jake eyes him. "You know what you're doing?"

"Two years of med school. I think I can manage."

I stand waiting as Triston attends to Jake's wound. And it does appease some of my anger as he pulls out a first aid kit, swabs the wound, which looks to be a surface wound only, and then stitches it up.

After he's bandaged it, he reaches into the kit and pulls out a few bottles of pills. "Antibiotics and painkillers. He'll be fine in a few days."

"Flesh wound," I affirm as I take the bottles.

"You're familiar?" he asks, cocking his head to the side.

"I'm a mafia princess," I retort, my voice full of acid.

He gives one nod. And then looks to Roman. "We should leave soon."

Roman jerks his chin, "That's my cue." And he starts for the door.

But I call him back. "Roman."

"Yes?"

"Who bought the Diamond?" I already know the answer.

Roman grimaces as he looks to Triston.

It's Triston who answers. "My family."

"Was that the deal? My life for a casino?" They are going to acknowledge it before this conversation continues.

But Triston doesn't answer. He doesn't want to answer for his brother's crimes, and I get that. Except I'm sure they all agreed to the plan.

"Just so we're clear..." I look to Roman first and then to Triston, "What happens next in Vegas happens with my help."

Jake shifts behind me and I turn to look at him. I'm about to make a major play here and say that I won't convince my cousins to side with the Kincaids. But I need to know that Jake and I are solid...

He gives me that half grin that I love. "Give him hell, baby girl."

That was all I needed to hear.

Did I ever worry if Jake was on my side? Never again.

Triston looks at Roman, who affirms my words with a nod. That one surprises me. I know Roman protected me today but this kind of support…

But Roman isn't done. "Our women are our center, and Nia is doubly so because she holds the keys to a great many opportunities."

Triston's mouth thins. "What is it you want, Nia?"

"I'm aware that the Diamond is yours. That was a deal made that I'm sure will be honored. But no further business is happening until your brother has settled up with me."

My hands come to my hips, my eyes shooting fire. "I love it when you're pissed, baby," Jake chuckles behind me.

I know he's seen flashes of this part of me and the fact that he doesn't just accept my power, but enjoys it…

I've never been more certain that Jake is the man for me.

Triston doesn't look at Roman or Jake, as he dips his chin in acknowledgment. "Your price?"

"I've got a plane ride to think it over." I take a seat, buckling my belt.

Roman gives me one last look, his eyes full of appreciation. "Nia, being a Kincaid looks good on you."

I smile back. I was a princess in my Italian family. But in this family of kings, I intend to be a queen. "Thank you, Roman."

I settle back. It's time to decide what I do with the Smiths.

CHAPTER THIRTY-SIX

JAKE

I WISH my arm didn't ache because I'd love to be buried balls-deep inside Nia. Christ, she's magnificent.

Those flashes of sass have become a crown of gold around her head. I'd heard her mutter...*from the ashes*.

She's going to breathe fire by the time she's done.

And she's going to put the Dukes exactly where they belong, while elevating our family. It's so odd, she was so intent upon getting out of this life, I never noticed how suited she was to it.

Killing Toni was self-defense. We could go to the law, and I'd never see the inside of a jail cell.

The cops were there when Toni tried to suffocate Nia so...

I have no doubt that Nia has the sort of ethics that will keep her on the right side of the law. But I also know that she isn't going to take shit from the Dukes or anyone else in this town.

She's just like me. A mix of the old school gangster, with the right amount of smarts that keep her on just this side of the moral line that will make sure we don't land in prison.

The plane takes off and I glance out the window at the burning car that we leave behind. Silence falls between us as the plane glides up to altitude.

"What price is Gris going to pay?" I ask, loving this plan. Because she's right. She has paid more than anyone ever should. I was shot because of my part. Gris won a major victory for his family, but he's got to ante up.

"Thoughts?" she asks me, running her fingers over my forearm. "I don't mean to make it hard for your family. But we can't keep doing business with them if I'm your wife. If Toni taught me one thing it's that getting your due respect carries the business a long way."

"He can pay you in real estate."

She nods. "Not bad. But there needs to a be a more personal element, I think."

"Digging the grave is a good one," I smile.

She smiles too. "Yeah?"

"Makes him take part in the dirty stuff you and I had to do." I wince, thinking of just how much she's suffered. Digging the hole isn't even close to good enough.

Nia taps her chin. "What did you say Mike does?"

"He's the head of security for the casino division."

Nia cocks her head. "And you are?"

I smile at her. "I run all of security. Clubs, casinos, personal. I'm Mike's boss."

Nia nods. "The Dukes will have to hire Mike to take over their casino security. For the Diamond."

I stare at her. "What?"

"It will elevate my sister and…" She gives me a wicked smile. "It gives us inside information on their business."

"Jesus Christ," I blink twice because it's absolutely brilliant. I pick up my phone to send a text to the family chat. One handed typing isn't usually my forte, but I manage with only a few typos.

. . .

NIA WANTS recompense from the Dukes. As my wife, she can't tolerate the slight. Her idea is to require the Dukes to hire Mike.

ROMAN IS the first to respond.

CAREFUL MASON. Nia might take over your job.

FUCK YOU, Roman. Mason replies, and then. *It's perfect.*

TO NIA, I add, "The Dukes want to purchase another of the old Italian casinos."

HER LIPS PURSE. "I don't think so."

I WONDER if my family is going to regret supporting Nia. I don't give a shit either way. No one understands me like Nia. We were made for each other. "Woman," I rumble because Nia isn't a girl any longer. "I'm going to need you to come over here and ride me like it's our last night on Earth."

"Jake," she gasps. "You're hurt and—"

"I'm just going to sit here. You're going to do all the real work," I reach my good arm toward her. "But I need to be inside you."

"How long is the flight?" She looks at the closed door to the cockpit.

"Another hour and a half at least," I answer.

With a quick nod, she stands up and yanks down her jeans, muttering. "I should have worn a dress."

I chuckle as I muscle my pants over my hips with one arm.

There is no foreplay, no warm-up as I rub spit on my cock a

second before Nia straddles me, sliding down my length until I'm buried inside her.

It's hot and fast and I barely feel the pain, as pleasure tightens my balls.

She cums with a scream and I instantly follow, my roar joining hers.

When she wilts against me, I wrap my arm around her, burying my face in her neck. "When are we going to make it official?" I ask when I'm able to speak again.

She pulls back, kissing my mouth. "Question first. Vegas chapel or big wedding?"

"Small wedding isn't an option?" I say, thinking back to Leo's ceremony. It was nice.

I'm still buried inside her. "An Italian would take the wedding and make it into a political spectacle, making all the other families pay homage."

I stare at her.

Roman might be right. Nia just might take his job after all…

EPILOGUE

Gris

My time in the gym is my sacred time…everyone in my family knows not to interrupt.

So when my phone rings for the third time, I'm naturally pissed.

I swear, all this Vegas sunshine makes me grumpy.

Who knew? I didn't think I'd miss London's rain, but there it's expected you'll just be a fucking prick.

Here in the states there is some expectation to be as happy as the weather. Americans.

Then again, I have more reason than usual to be miserable. Some of our major plans with the Kincaids are falling to shit….

Which is what causes me to finally pick up my ringing phone.

My brother Tris's name flashes on the screen, which only deepens my impending dread. I hit the call button. "Tris."

"Gris," he answers back. "Sorry to interrupt your workout time."

I don't answer. There is no need. He wouldn't be calling if it wasn't important. "I've got news on the Kincaid front," he starts with a sigh.

My stomach tightens. "I'm sure I already know what you're going to say—"

"Did you talk to Roman?"

"Roman?" I stare down at the phone. What the fuck is he talking about? "I thought you said you knew. Why would I have spoken to Roman?"

Tris is silent. "I think we'd both better start talking."

"Go," I answer. "You called me so it must be important."

"Toni Carcetti is dead."

"Fuck," Yeah, that is important. "How?"

"Jake Kincaid shot him in self-defense."

My eyes close as I sit down on the weight bench behind me. "Tell me more."

In clipped tones my brother explains how Toni attempted to kill his own daughter, the daughter I sent to the Kincaids, and how Jake defended her, not once but twice.

"He's marrying her, Gris."

My stomach clenches. "Who is marrying whom?" I already know, but it's bad enough that my head falls into my hand.

"Jake is marrying Nia. Can you believe that? From kidnap victim to queen."

Fuck. Me.

"Any chance we can break them up?" I know it's a shit thing to say but I am the man who set Nia up. I played her like a fucking pawn and now she's the queen on the board, free to come at me with whatever moves she chooses.

"I heard them fuck on the plane. You'd have to kill Jake and then the rest of the Kincaids would take all their might and power to come after you, after us."

I draw in a deep breath of air, trying to clear my head. Think. "So…what happens next?"

"Fuck if I know," Tris sounds as tired as I feel. "But she's really pissed, and she claims that Jake has paid his debt to her, but you…"

I stare down at the phone. "And what about Mason? He's going to let her dictate these kinds of things?"

"Yeah. She's delivering the entire Italian empire to him without a single law broken or another drop of blood spilled, from what I can tell. She's far more useful than us, honestly, and I could hear in Jake's voice that even if she wasn't, he'll back her to the death."

"Fuck," I rumble out, my fist driving into the padded bench I sit on.

"You hand-delivered a beautiful woman, a mafia princess, into the arms of the Kincaids. You had to know this was a move that could backfire. She used her God-given gifts to outplay you, Gris."

He's not wrong. Nia is a looker, and unlike her sister, Nia's clear blue eyes shine with intelligence and fire.

"So what is she demanding?"

"I don't know yet, but if I were to guess, I'd say castration of one kind or another."

I punch the bench again, my fingers near breaking as pain shoots up my arm.

Then I draw in another long gulp of air. Because this game isn't over yet… "Ready for my news?"

"You don't want to keep talking about Nia?"

"Roman and Luke are missing."

"What?" he rumbles out into the phone. "You can't be serious?"

"I am. Serious. Last anyone heard, they had gone to this vacant lot that they were trying to purchase for their tunnel project. They need the piece of land for ventilation."

"When was that?"

"Wee hours of the morning," I answer. "The car was there when the sun came up, but both men are gone."

"Dead?" he asks, and I hear him run his hand over his scruff.

"I don't know." I hope not. I like them both. But I might hate Vegas. For all the talk of being a shiny, happy place, the filth runs deep.

"So…are the Kincaids about to implode?"

I don't answer right away. Mason is the brains and Leo is the muscle. Jake is the old-school gangster who keeps them just enough in the gray. Can the three of them do this on their own? "I doubt it. Mason, Leo, and Jake have got what it takes."

"So we help…" Tris answers. "And we win back their good grace."

We help.

Rolling my shoulders I stand up from the bench. My uncle is the Duke of Highgrove. But we're born from a time when our family participated in every illegal vice known to Britain to fight and claw our way to the top of society.

It's a fact that usually disappears from a family's memory, but not in our case.

And it's something that the Kincaids couldn't possibly understand.

When it comes to being a gangster, we are the originals.

And it's time to fight dirty…

OH MY GOD.... Is anyone as excited as I am for the next installment of the "Lords of Las Vegas?"

Obviously, Roman and Luke are next. Keep reading if you want a sneak peek of where they are and how their stories are going to begin.

King of Ruin *and* **King of Pain** *will be launching in late 2024 and early 2025.*

But just in case you were wondering, the "Lords of Las Vegas" does not end with Roman and Luke. The Smiths will be the next family to be featured beginning with Gris and Tris. So buckle up...these Dukes are revving their engines!

Coming starting in 2025!!!

Duke of Depravity

KING OF RUIN

LORDS OF LAS VEGAS

I might be BLIND, but I still should have SEEN that he was trouble.
A scheming billionaire perched on the brink of dominance.

Cold
Calculating
Ruthless
A king

Roman Kincaid is everything I'm not... He's a King. A god among men.

A man who owns the entire world. Almost...

Despite being handicapped, and the caretaker of every wounded animal that comes my way, it does not exempt me from catching his attention.

Though I can't make out the color of his eyes, I can still feel their heat.

Because I've got something he wants.

A little piece of land, my own sanctuary that I use to look after my little patients.

But it turns out that one little piece of land, the one thing that's mine, is the very thing he needs.

And there isn't anything he won't do to get it.

He's not the only one.

His enemies want it too. Which means, I'm caught in their war.

And just because there is an attraction that simmers between Roman and me, that doesn't make him my protector. A good guy.

He is not a hero.

Roman Kincaid is a predator.

And just like the little birds I care for, I have always just been Roman Kincaid's….

Prey.

KING OF RUIN

Roman

The blades of the helicopter are still whirring over my head as we exit the chopper at the top of Kincaid Tower.

What a fucking day.

From our vantage point, I can see all the lights of Vegas spread out before us. The city glitzes and shimmers like the grand illusion that it is. Meant to be an oasis, it's just as lethal as the desert beyond.

I'd hoped to get back sooner.

But we'd had Nia and Jake to see off on their trip to the Keys, and then there had been the car to deal with….

It takes a bit of time to dispose of a burnt-out wreck with bullet holes.

And of course, there was the body…

I scrub a hand through my hair as my cousin Luke pushes a button on his phone, unlocking the rooftop door to the private elevator.

"I got seven calls while we were in flight," he growls out as the door opens and we step into the elevator.

"Any of them the police?" I ask, my eyes closing as I lean against the wall, exhaustion pulling at my limbs.

"No. Just the fucking building inspector, and my lead architect, and the foreman of the construction crew. Fuck me."

The moment the doors slide open to the conference room, he's got his phone to his ear, snarling words I only half listen to as I pour myself a glass of scotch from the bar at the far end of the room.

In theory, my brothers, my cousin Luke, and my uncle Jake, are the five owners of a successful real estate enterprise.

But we are also the five fingers of a fist.

And no one gets to where we are without getting their hands dirty.

I take a large swallow of the drink and then another, I don't love these days. The days where I'm not in the boardroom but fighting off Italian Mafia as they try to take what is ours with guns instead of corporate mergers.

But either way, we do what we have to do to stay on top.

My phone rings, my brother Mason's name popping up on the screen. I take another swallow and pick up. "Mason."

"What the fuck happened today?"

"Toni's dead, Jake is wounded, and Nia is on the warpath." And then I finish the glass and pour another.

"Toni's dead?"

"Yeah. Tweedle Dee and Tweedle Dum Vendetti were with him, though, and they both got away."

"Those are two problems we're going to need to solve soon. Tell me about Nia."

"I think the Vendetti twins are going to be the much easier discussion."

Mason sighs. "Tell me about Nia anyway."

"Our new aunt," I say with a snort because while Jake is pushing forty, Nia is younger than all of us, "would like some recompense from Gris Smith. In her words, she's paid a hefty price to become part of this family. And Jake just had to kill her father to keep her safe. But she feels that Gris has been all gain and no pain after the way he set her up and it's time he put his skin in the game. She's not wrong."

Mason grunts. "Should have seen that one coming."

And that's why Mason is our fearless leader. He rarely misses a move and blames himself when he does. "Her exact words to Gris's brother were, and I'm quoting, 'I'm a mafia princess who is now a queen of Vegas. You didn't think what your brother did was going to go unpunished?'"

"What did Jake say?" Mason asks, not commenting on Nia at all. He's calculating the damage and how to spin this to our advantage, I know it.

"He said, 'Give him hell, baby girl,'" I repeat. Jake was completely behind his woman. Which I understand. Nia is as beautiful as she was vulnerable, and Jake has been hooked about as deeply as a man can be.

She's not so vulnerable anymore. Jake has gone about eliminating her problems one body at a time.

Hence why I was on clean-up duty today.

"And Triston Smith? What was his response?"

"It seems like he's going to make his brother pay whatever price Nia demands."

"She's a businesswoman underneath the bombshell exterior," Mason murmurs. "She negotiated with me like a pro."

"That is true."

"Shit. I'm getting a text from Jake now." He pauses, likely reading the message.

"He says that Nia's decided on her demand of the Smiths: put our casino security man in charge of his casinos too. Eyes and ears right on every one of their floors."

I pull the phone away from my ear and stare at it. Christ. It's a brilliant plan. "Wow," I mutter.

"I know. She's making us stronger."

"Remind me not to piss her off," I respond, though I know I pissed her off already. She was our enemy's daughter.

But then again, it's kind of a me problem. I don't seem to know where to draw lines with women.

In my defense, my mother died when I was young.

I only remember her as the sweet-smelling woman who gave the best hugs. As a man, I know women are far more complex with weapons all their own.

Nia is the perfect example of that.

A woman who looked weak but is rising like the tide and growing stronger by the day.

I take another swallow of my drink, knowing I ought to slow down. But the past few days have unsettled some careful balance I usually keep.

"Fuck," Luke yells from the next room, loud enough that Mason hears him too.

"What's happening?" Mason asks.

Instead of answering, I switch the phone to speaker and cross the conference room to the adjoining meeting room.

Luke is standing by the windows, his back stiff and straight, his jaw clenched in hard lines. "How much did you offer her?" he asks in clipped tones.

My brow furrows as I cock my head as I listen.

"And she didn't take it?"

Mason is silent, surely listening too.

"Make her another offer, double it." Luke's hand slices through the air like he'd like to cut all this bullshit.

"Why wouldn't she take it?" He looks back at me, his brow slashed in an angry line as he listens to the speaker on the other end of the phone. "Are you fucking kidding me?" He spits.

"What's wrong?" I finally ask, not that he answers.

"Tell me you're researching her. Find a weakness, find a way to make sure she sells." And then he hangs up.

I wait, not one to repeat myself, as he drops his phone in his pocket and scrubs his face.

Letting out a long breath of air, he finally grunts. "Problem with the tunnel."

"What problem?" Mason asks.

Luke eyes my phone like I've betrayed him. Did he not want Mason to hear this? That's too bad. We don't keep secrets from each other.

"The problem is that there aren't enough ventilation vents in the tunnel and the place they've requested we add one is underneath the land of a small nonprofit animal sanctuary."

Small animal sanctuary? In the city?

"Judging by what I heard," Mason clears his throat. "Offers have been made but she's refusing to part with the land?"

"That's right," Luke nods, looking at me.

I set down my glass and scrub a hand across my jaw. "We'll take a look at the property. See what size it is, what facilities she's got. My guess is if we offered a larger parcel with more amenities somewhere else, she'd take it."

Luke's eyes light up.

"I agree," Mason rumbles. "The sooner the better. We could do with a few less problems."

We certainly could.

I hang up with Mason and pick up my glass, draining the drink. "First thing tomorrow?" I ask, wishing for nothing more than the bliss of my quiet apartment and the comfort of my bed.

Luke shakes his head. "I'm not sleeping tonight. I think I'll go now."

"You can't show up at a woman's place at one in the morning without ending up in a cell."

"I just want to do a drive by and it's a business not a home."

I scowl. "I'm going to bed, and I'm not picking up my phone, so if you end up in jail, I'm not bailing you out tonight."

"You're not coming with me?" Luke asks with a frown. "I could use your eyes on this one. Without the vent, the project will be stalled for months. Our first permits are running out the end of this week."

I mutter several curses because that's Luke. Leaving out important information and running things down to the wire. "I hate you right now."

"But you'll come?"

I let out a long breath of air as I look down at the second glass of scotch I just finished.

Maybe it's the drinks, or the hellish day but a sense of dread fills me. "Fine, asshole."

"Thanks, dickhead."

He strides toward the elevator. "I'll drive."

I set down the glass and follow behind him. "What do we know about this woman?"

"It's some hippie, I think. She takes the birds that get wounded running into the skyscrapers and doctors them."

This is decent information. She'll want to be close to the city. "This hippie have a name?"

"Maddie Fox." Luke presses the button at least a dozen times as we wait for the doors to open. "It's a tiny tenth of an acre parcel but she's refusing to sell, despite the offer being four times the value of the property."

I frown as I take in that particular piece of information. "Either she's crazy or she's got some ulterior motive."

Luke shakes his head. "I agree. Which is why I want to gather a bit of information when I can assess the property without being observed."

The elevator opens and I give him a long glare as we step in. "I've had enough shady dealings for today."

"I'm not going to be shady." He doesn't meet my eye.

"Bullshit."

"Ok, I'm not going to get caught. Besides, we both know a woman like that does not have cameras."

I shake my head, knowing I'm going to regret this as the elevator stops at the garage and we walk toward Luke's Ferrari.

The drive is short, her small parcel right in the heart of the city. How she's kept it for this long is rather impressive.

We get out of the car, the flickering streetlight only making me more certain I've made a mistake. The alcohol is taking effect, and my senses are dimmed as I take in the street. We're on the back side of several casinos where traffic is more limited.

Her lot is protected by six-foot-high brick walls, not that Luke cares.

Before I've said a word, he takes a three-step running leap and vaults over the top. "You're a billionaire who wears a suit most days. What the fuck are you doing?"

"I'm a man who gets the job done," he calls from the other side of the wall.

Several birds squawk in response and I roll my eyes. "What you're doing is your best to get arrested."

But I stop talking, letting him do his thing as I watch the street.

I do manage to note that the walled yard is attached to a stucco building that looks like it might be a two-family residence. Another Vegas oddity.

No lights are on inside, but I have this moment of unease. Does Maddie Fox live there? Is that why she won't sell?

I cock my head to the side. "Luke," I rumble out in a rough whisper. I'm liking this less and less.

He hops back over the wall. "She's got about thirty birds and a few squirrels. That's what's holding up our billion-dollar project. A few parakeets."

"Parakeets don't fly into buildings, they live in them around here," I answer automatically. Something isn't right. I can feel it.

"Seriously, though. Why won't she sell?"

That's when I see the headlights coming around the corner. I step back into the shadow of the wall, my arm flinging out, to push Luke back too.

"Fuck," he mutters as the car not only comes toward us but stops right in front of the house.

"You packing?" I ask, realizing that I'm not.

"No," he spits. "Shit."

We're hidden, but his car is in plain view.

The driver gets out of the car and opens the rear door behind him, helping someone from the car.

Even in this light, I catch the flash of long blonde hair as the man slips a hand around her waist, walking her toward the door.

There is something familiar about the guy, and I lean closer. If I'd skipped the scotch, I'm sure I'd already know what's making the hair on the back of my neck stand up.

"Fuck me, that's Vigo Vendetti," Luke mutters.

The passenger door opens too, and I know that Luke is correct. Because Vincent Vendetti is walking straight toward us.

This is bad.

The Vendettis are the unhinged nephews of the man we killed today. And if they realize that the Ferrari is Luke's, they've got us right where they want us…

I lean closer to the wall, my jaw hard as granite. "What do you want to do?"

I hear Luke growl. "We can make a break for the car, or we can…

But Vincent's scanning the area and I swear, he sees me, our eyes locking.

My hand comes to my chest, feeling the bulletproof layer of protection I've been wearing since this morning.

It only takes a second for Vincent to reach behind him and pull out a pistol.

I barely hear the two pops before I feel the bullet strike my shoulder. I look over just in time to see Luke go down…

Want to read more? King of Ruin

STALK ME LIKE AN ALPHA!

Join my newsletter to get all the latest updates!

Tammy's Newsletter

And follow me everywhere else for teasers, giveaway, book news and fun!

www.authortammyandresen.com
www.facebook.com/authortammyandresen
www.instagram.com/tammyandresen
https://www.tiktok.com/@lordsoflasvegas
www://amazon.com/authortammyandresen

MORE ABOUT TAMMY

Tammy is the writer of Bestselling Regency Romance who could not resist the urge of writing in the dark and delicious world of Contemporary Dark and Steamy Billionaire Romance.

She lives with her husband and three children in Massachusetts and her favorite adventures are the ones that are found in books but occasionally she lives a few of her own!

Made in the USA
Las Vegas, NV
24 May 2026